Holy Deception

Jessica A. Robinson

Giving Your Soul a Rise...One Page at a Time

ISBN-13: 978-0692257784
ISBN-10: 0692257780

PEACE IN THE STORM PUBLISHING, LLC.
P.O. Box 1152
Pocono Summit, PA 18346

Visit our Web site at
www.PeaceInTheStormPublishing.com

Holy Deception

by Jessica A. Robinson

Acknowledgements

As I sit down to write out my acknowledgements I am in a true state of gratitude and appreciation to so many people in my life.

First and foremost I would like to thank God. He has blessed me with the ability to touch the world through written word and for that I am forever grateful. I don't take my gift lightly or for granted.

To the Robinson, Oliver, Moore-Yuille, Miles, Graves and Thornton Families, Although there are too many to name individually I have been influenced by each and every one of you and the imprint left on my heart cannot be replaced.

Gabriel, Michael, Britney, & Dominique I love you all more than you know. It brings me great joy to see you all embarking on your new journey together. I'm just a phone call away if you need me.

Terrence, You are the love of my life. I thank God for you every single day. You have made these past three years the best years of my entire life. So grateful to be on this journey called life together. I love your children as if they were my own. Chimarra B. & Xavier P. I love you guys!

Arlene Beaver, Martha Taylor, Lois Hines, Rhonda Padrutt, Lorraine Hardman, Sandra Robinson, Crystal Robinson, Deborah Robinson, and Alisa Tarver I draw a maternal strength from you all that is amazing and even though my actual mother isn't here I thank God that you all are here bridging the gap that was left since she made her transition to heaven. I just simply want to say thank you.

Special thanks to the absolute greatest publisher in

the world Elissa Gabrielle. You believed in me before I had ever written a single word and here we are four books later. I'm truly thankful for you and the entire PITS family.

Rebecca Grubbs & Dinesha (Dee) Robinson, my friendships couldn't have come at a better time. You two are more like sisters than friends. Love yall.

Sarah, Leslie, Allyson Tasha, Janelle, Schannel, and Joi, I love you all. Thanks for friendship and sisterhood that have stood the test of time.

Maurice Gooch, thank you always doing such an awesome job on my hair and styling me for all my events. You are truly a visionary and the best at what you do.

Vida Baldwin, thanks for a dope cover as well as a hot website to match. You are truly the best at what you do.

Rhonda Crowder, thank you for the constant push to make me a better writer. I am grateful for your honesty and expertise all of which has caused me to grow leaps and bounds as a writer.

Kisha Green, Lutishia Lovely, Allyson Imes, Isaiah David Paul, Julia "Press" Simmons, Angel Mechelle, Allison Grace, Tanisha Pettiford, Kimyatta, T. Styles, Charisse: Thanks for all your support and encouragement in the literary industry. I am so glad to have real friends in this industry because the fakes come a dime a dozen nowadays. If I have forgotten anyone please charge it to my head and not my heart. I'll be sure to catch you on the next one.

Peace & Blessings,
Jessica A. Robinson

Dedication

This book is dedicated to two very special people in my life. First I would like to dedicate my fourth novel to my grandmother Ruth Moore Robinson affectionately known as my "twin." Thank you for always taking time out with me to show me how to really be a woman with morals, goals, and have a personal relationship with Jesus Christ. I will never forget how beautiful of a person you were and the many sleepovers we had at your house on Colby Street. I love you so very much and strive to make you forever proud.

Mohammed Hassen aka "Mo", you were such a great guy. I am glad that God allowed us to meet when we were little. You were truly an awesome husband, father and friend. Even though you left us suddenly, I am reassured that you are in a better place. I ultimately know God only takes the absolute best to be with him. Miss you my friend. Rest in Heaven.

Personal from the First Lady herself:

So here we have a third book written about yours truly... even though I am highly upset, I am secretly flattered that this author thinks enough about me to write multiple books. Even though the majority of what you're reading about me is lies and full of embellishment, it's still about me. I can't tell you how many emails I've sent her and how many times I've hacked her Facebook page to make sure she knew I wasn't playing with her at all. If she insists on writing stories about me, they should at least want it to be the truth. So when I finally caught up with her, I confronted her and she finally sees things my way so you guys can know the truth. I haven't read the final version of this book but what I've been allowed to read seems to be pretty accurate so without further ado sit back, relax and enjoy Holy Deception!

Your favorite First Lady,
Denise Tate

Prologue

Denise

❝❝I really can't believe you and Kaylah are moving," Terri said as she playfully bounced Kaylah on her knee. The baby began to laugh uncontrollably as they played.

"Well believe it, Terri, because we are moving. Everything is already set and, once we're ready to board our flight, me and baby girl are off to start our new life."

Terri really didn't want Kaylah and I to move out of state but I've been telling her for months that we were getting the heck out of Youngstown. Regardless if she believed me or not, my mind was made up and there was no turning back. After all that craziness with Myra, Tyrone's sister, trying to kill me, my marriage to Randy never recovered. By the time I made it out of the hospital, Randy had already begun the preliminary paperwork to divorce me. There was nothing I could do or say. It was like talking to a brick wall. I had really messed up and in turn lost a really great man behind my own foolishness.

For the past year, we have been working through the divorce proceedings and tying up all of the loose ends. With a whole twelve months of pulling all stops, trying to win him back, my pleas of forgiveness falling on deaf ears and a cold heart, I decided to pack my things and go. Randy gave me the house but the longer I stayed there, the more I thought about how permanent our divorce became. It drove me crazy to be in that house day in and day out. So after three months, I decided to put it on the market and rented a condo around the corner. Without Randy, the house didn't feel like a home anymore. He got mad when he heard about me selling our house but, since he left it to me, there wasn't anything he could do to change my mind. The house sold within four months and I had enough money to start a brand new life somewhere else.

"I totally understand. But do you have to go all the way to Florida to start over?" Terri asked.

"I feel like that's where God is calling me to go. I know it's difficult but we'll be back to visit. This isn't goodbye. It's more like see you later," I replied. Terri had to accept the reality of it all. I was getting the heck up out of Youngstown. With the latest scandal that hit our church, I truly had too many enemies to count and I felt it would be better if I removed myself rather than deal with all the scrutiny I'd faced in the past year. It literally felt like the girl who wore the scarlet letter. Everywhere I went, there was someone who had something to say about me. If they weren't talking out loud, they were whispering behind my back and I was way too fabulous to live a life like that. It was funny how, in the church, we were taught to forgive and overlook people's indiscretions but were the main ones to remind people of their mistakes. I desperately tried to move on but everyone around me made it difficult. I received harassing phone calls on my cell phone practically all day long. Random people texted me, calling me all kinds of names. Everything but a child of God. Not to mention the looks and stares that I got when I went to church every Sunday. After a few months of the public ridicule, I decided to stop attending Oakdale Baptist. I believe it was for the best.

"I know you're not leaving forever. You better come back and visit and, when Carlos and I take our vacation this year, we want to take Kaylah to Disney World. We were just talking about that on our flight home."

"That's fine with me. You can come and get Kaylah whenever you would like. She's in the terrible twos and I can't wait for her little behind to be three. So enough about us. How was the honeymoon?" I smiled as I looked down at my daughter, now looking at me. She had been giving me the blues for the past six months and I couldn't wait for her to pass through this stage.

"Girl, St. Tropez was absolutely beautiful. Out of all the places I've been in my life, it has to be the most breathtaking. Carlos agreed." Terri smiled and then released a little naughty smirk, suggesting they truly enjoyed each other.

"I'm so happy for you guys. How's married life treating you?" I asked.

"Wonderful, I love it. It's totally different having someone to come home to every night and I wouldn't trade it for the world. I just wished things could be different with you and Randy. You two were the initial reason why I believed in love in the first place."

"Honey, it's okay. Things happen for a reason and while I would love to still be married to him and living here I realize that things have definitely changed." Just then I checked the flight schedule and realized it was time for my daughter and I to make our way through TSA if we wanted to make our flight on time. I was glad it was time for us to go. Even though I loved talking to my best friend, I was tired of talking about Randy and wishing things were different. As far as I was concerned, he decided to walk away from our marriage. He opted out of our relationship so it was time for me to move on. We were divorced and there wasn't no changing that. I had even heard through the grapevine that he'd begun dating his old flame Alexis. I knew that tramp wasn't all innocent as she appeared to. She had her eyes out for my man from day one and probably shouted for joy once she heard of my relationship's demise. I hadn't actually seen them out together but a little birdie told me they had seen them a few times walking through the mall and at dinner. I didn't regret leaving at all. It was time for me to go. I had outgrown Youngstown. It was time for me to spread my wings elsewhere.

"So I'm not gonna say goodbye. It's more like I will see you later." Terri grabbed me and gave me the biggest hug ever. For a second she was about to make me cry but I did my best to hold it all together.

"Ti-Ti pick me up!" Kaylah demanded. She called Terri Ti-Ti since she couldn't fully say Aunt Terri. It always made my best friend smile although this time it darn near brought her to tears. She did as Kaylah requested. She picked her up and swung her around in the air and gave her multiple kisses before she put her down. I picked up my purse and our carry-on bag and we started to walk toward the long security line.

"Well I think if I hug you again I will break down and cry so why don't you just promise me you'll call me once you land and get settled." Terri said as I handed the woman at the desk our tickets.

"You know I will call you as soon as we get there. I love you." I replied as Kaylah and I started to walk through the metal detectors and out of sight of Terri who stood there waving and blowing her goddaughter kisses. I had such a good feeling as we got closer and closer to boarding our seats on the plane. You know that feeling that you get when you feel like something great is about to happen? Well I literally had butterflies as the flight attendant showed me our first-class seats. I let Kaylah take the window seat because she was absolutely fascinated with planes and flying. It was like the girl had no fear at all. I took the seat right next to her and the row directly across from me was empty. I didn't pay any attention to it. I reached in our carry-on bag and pulled out Kaylah's iPad and headphones. Between the view from the window and her tablet she would be busy. With my daughter preoccupied, I decided to pull out my mirror and make sure my appearance was on point. I had chopped all of my hair off when I visited my hair stylist for the last time.

That served as the beginning of the new me. After eyeing myself in the mirror, I realized the only thing I was missing was a fresh coat of MAC lipstick. I pulled out my *Quite the Thing* lipstick and made sure my lips were evenly covered with my favorite shade of magenta.

"Excuse me do you know if that seat is taken?" A man asked as he approached the seats across the aisle from me. I looked over and shook my head.

"No one's sitting there. I haven't seen anyone since we got on the plane." I smiled.

"It's okay. I was worried I had the wrong seat. But I'm glad that I was wrong." He smiled back. This man looked absolutely gorgeous. I became lost in his hazel eyes and mocha-brown complexion. His pearly white teeth and dimples seemed mesmerizing. I know he probably thought I was crazy by the way I stared but he looked so familiar to me. I felt like I knew him or had saw him somewhere. When he sat down, his *Dolce & Gabbana* cologne invaded my nostrils and entered me into a fragrant trance. His D-Squared dress shirt with silver diamond cuff links and True Religion jeans said he had excellent taste when it came to clothes. He definitely had a distinctive style like no other. And even though I took notice of his intoxicating presence, I didn't let him know how I felt. Instead I pulled out my Kindle Fire and started reading a book I had just purchased from Amazon. I paid him no attention as I started to get into *Sex in the Sanctuary by Lutishia Lovely*. But out of the corner of my eye, I could feel him staring at me.

"Please stop me if I'm being too forward but what is a beautiful woman like you doing traveling all alone?"

He asked as he took off his jacket and draped it over the back of his seat.

"If that was your way of trying to figure out if I was single or not then you're real clever." I smiled at him and then looked over at Kaylah, who hung on to his every word. I pulled up a game on her tablet which was her cue to start playing it and quit being so nosey.

"Well if you must know my daughter and I are on our way to our new home in Florida," I replied.

"That's actually where I'm on my way to as well."

"Oh I bet you can't wait to get home to your wife and kids." I smiled and waited for him to confirm what I already sensed.

"I don't have a wife or any kids. Travelling the country as a full-time evangelist affords me with very little time to myself."

That's when it hit me. I had seen him on TV more times than I could count.

"You're D.J. Rogers! You're the one always on the Light Network." His eyes lit up as I uttered his name.

"Yes that's me. So you've seen me on the Light?"

"Once or twice." I replied, lying. The truth was I've seen him on the show more times than I could count but I would never tell him that. It seemed like he wanted me to shower him with compliments to boost his little Holy Ghost ego. I was determined to play it cool the entire way.

D.J. shook his head and smiled at me. "So, you said you're on your way to your new home in Florida. I hope I'm not being too forward by asking you what area of Florida are you moving to?"

"My baby girl and I are moving to Orlando."

"That's where I live. The church I attend is there too." He smiled.

"This is a definitely a small world."

"Well I always say, nothing happens by happenstance. Every moment we experience and every person we encounter is all for a reason. So I would like to think we were meant to be on the same flight travelling the same way and sitting directly next to each other. This is nothing but God setting us up." He pressed his lips together revealing a set of dimples that would make the prettiest woman jealous.

"So you think God has set us up, huh?" I asked as I laughed a little. His revelation caught me off guard slightly.

"I believe that. But whatever reason he allowed us to cross paths, I'm open to it." He winked at me.

"I'm open as well." I blushed then he leaned in a little closer to me.

"I am really going to enjoy this flight home."

As I stared at this gorgeous man, looking at me like he wanted to devour me right then and there, I must admit that I was going to enjoy this flight too. I had a feeling that life as I knew it would never be the same.

Chapter 1

Denise

As Donovan and I waited for our flight to clear for take-off, my mind thought back to the conversation my mother and I just had recently. "Denise, are you being serious right now?" My mother yelled into the phone. I called her as soon as Donovan proposed to me. He proposed six months after we met. I had hoped she would be happy.

"Don't you think your rushing things?" She continued. " I mean you two just met each other. Why are you in a rush to get married again?"

"We're not rushing at all. Donovan said that the Lord spoke to him. Told him that I'm his wife. We both love each other and feel there is no need to wait"

"Okay Denise you know what's best for you. I just want you to really think about this before you just jump and get married."

That following week, she flew down to Florida to meet him and was impressed. We took her to lunch. By the time our bill came, she fell in love with him.

I know that marrying someone that I've literally only spent three or four days with over the course of six months could be considered irrational and even stupid but I've never been so sure of someone in my entire life. Because he travelled so much around the country, we were only able to spend his off days together. When we were together everything felt so right.

Terri, on the other hand, never met him so she planned to be one of our witnesses at the ceremony. I couldn't wait for them two to meet. Up until this point, they had only talked over the phone.

"So tell me how do you feel about coming in to Vegas at night?" Donovan asked, snapping me out of my daydream. I looked over at him.

"Baby, this is absolutely beautiful. And flying in on your private jet couldn't get any better," I replied.

"I told you this was the best time to fly into the city. It's an entirely different experience." He replied then glanced down at his phone. He put it back into his pocket.

"Who was that honey?" I looked at Donovan who wore the most puzzling look on his face.

"I dunno babe. I didn't recognize the number."

No sooner than he finished that statement, his phone rang again. And again. And again. He continued to ignore it.

"Why don't you just answer it? Who keeps trying

to call you?" He looked irritated.

"I'm not sure, honey. They must have the wrong number because I never get phone calls from numbers I don't recognize. Don't worry, this is our weekend baby. I will worry about answering my phone when we get back home." He leaned in and planted a kiss on my cheek. God! This man knew how to send chills up and down my spine with the slightest touch. People may call me crazy for running off to elope with Donovan but I felt like I was making the right choice.

By the time our flight landed at the airport, butterflies began to form in my stomach. Everything started to become even more real than it previously had. We weren't just talking about eloping anymore. It was actually taking place right before my very eyes. Even though I was sure of the decision, I still couldn't prevent my nerves for trying to get the best of me. To tell the truth, I wasn't even trying to get married. But I'm not getting any younger and having such a high profiled man interested in yours truly sealed the deal for me. Being with Donovan surely beat being alone and playing the single mother role.

Yes, we didn't actually know each other in and out but we knew enough to take this relationship to the next level. I even prayed before we decided to come out here and asked God to align our plans if this marriage was meant to be. Donovan took the lead when it came to planning our wedding ceremony and I even got Randy to fly to Orlando to get Kaylah for two weeks. I took all of that as a true sign that I was supposed to become Mrs. Donovan Rodgers.

Donovan and I chose Las Vegas as the perfect

destination to say "I do" because I had already been married and didn't want a big ceremony anyway. It wasn't about the ceremony. It was more about our relationship and our marriage over anything else. Donovan shared the same exact views I did. He wanted something nice, intimate, and private. With him being in the spotlight all of the time, he has never been afforded the luxury of privacy.

"What time will your best friend arrive?" He asked.

"I just texted her. She said they will be arriving later tonight. She will call us once they arrive at the hotel."

"That's great. Can you believe in less than 48 hours you will be my wife?" He smiled, causing me to blush.

"I know. I can't believe it but I do know that I'm ready." I leaned in and kissed him. For a moment, it felt like heaven. Until his phone interrupted our moment of temporary bliss. He tried to ignore the buzzing but it vibrated so many times that I could feel it.

"Babe, your phone."

"What about it?" he asked as if totally oblivious

"It's been vibrating non-stop for the last few minutes. Aren't you gonna answer it?" I asked him.

"No, whoever it is will have to wait. This weekend is all about you and me. I don't care who is trying to call me. I'm putting the whole world on hold for you this weekend. This is all about you and me and no one else. I'm turning my phone off right now."

Just hearing him say this, made me feel like the most special woman in the world. Nothing else mattered.

Chapter 2

Denise

A loud knock on our suite door woke me. Donovan remained snoring next to me. I nudged him.

"Babe, who do you think is at the door so God awful early?" I sat up in bed.

"I dunno baby. Maybe they got the wrong room." He yawned and then rolled over. I tried to lay back down in bed and get comfortable but, soon as I found a cozy spot, the knocking continued.

"I'm going to go see who it is." I got out of bed, put on my silk robe and made my way to the door. I opened it to see a man standing in front of me with two dozen long stemmed roses.

"These are for you Mrs. Rodgers." The man said. Just hearing him refer to me as such made me smile. I allowed him to walk past so he could set the flowers on the table. By the time I made it back to our bedroom, Donovan was sitting up on the side of the bed laughing. He held a small teal box in his hand.

"You knew all along." I said as I playfully hit his arm.

"Yes. And if I would've told you, I would've given away the surprise."

"Thank you for the flowers baby. They are absolutely beautiful."

"You're welcome. And this is also for you." He presented me with the tiny box and I almost completely destroyed it out of pure excitement.

"Oh my God! These earrings are amazing!"

"I'm glad you love them. Baby, I just want to give you the world. I know after Randy did all those horrible things to you and divorced you that you gave up on love. I just want to be the man that makes you believe in love all over again."

Donovan pulled me in close to him and hugged me tight. I'm glad he couldn't see my face because, every time he brought up my situation with Randy, it caused me to twinge a little bit. I know Randy hasn't done anything remotely close to what I claimed but I had to give a more valid reason for my marriage ending other than my unfaithful ways. I couldn't be completely honest with him especially since I desired to be Donovan's wife. I did what I had to do in this situation. Besides it wasn't like we ran the risk of bumping into Randy around town. I lived in an entirely different state and their actual contact with each other would be minimal to none.

"You seem excited but how do you really feel now that you're getting married to Donovan?" Terri asked me as we sat across from each other at a nearby nail salon. We decided to meet up and have a little day of pampering before the ceremony. It felt so good to be spending time with my best friend. I hadn't seen her since Kaylah and I moved to Florida a year ago.

"Girl, I'm literally over the moon. This man has done nothing but shower me with gifts since we got off the plane." I smiled and showed off my newest gift, the pair of diamond earrings he just gave me.

"Girl, those earrings look amazing on you," Terri said as the nail technician led us into the pedicure area where we sat in chairs next to each other.

"Thanks! My man definitely has taste."

"Apparently. With all the money he makes, I know your shopping addiction is going to be out of control."

"Already is. He messed around and gave me a black card last week." I smiled wide. I exposed every single one of my teeth and I didn't care not in the least bit. For once in my life, I felt like I was with someone on the same level as me.

"So how does Randy feel about you tying the knot?"

"Terri, in all honesty, this has nothing to do with Randy. And if you want to know, I didn't tell him anything. All he would do is have something negative to say like he does about everything else I choose to do. I don't have time for that foolishness right now." I rolled my eyes.

"So I see you two are still at odds with each other huh?"

"When are we not at odds with each other? Randy's still pissed I moved so far away. Gonna have the nerve to tell me I did it just to spite him."

"He said that for real?"

"Girl, yeah. I almost came through the phone on that fool."

"That's crazy. I didn't expect him to say anything like that at all."

"Well it definitely doesn't surprise me. He's jealous I actually moved on with my life. But what does he expect me to do? He's the one who divorced me not vice versa. Knowing him, he probably wanted me to be laid out on his doorstep begging for him to take me back but that's never been me. I've never been a beggar."

"I totally understand."

"And as far as I'm concerned, my marriage and my man is none of his business."

"Girl, when Randy finds out, he's gonna blow a freaking blood gasket."

I shrugged my shoulders. "So. I don't care. Maybe he'll realize he should've never been so quick to divorce me whatever he feels is not my concern anymore."

I believed I was completely justified in not telling Randy. It's not like he actually called me and gave me a play by play on his life and his relationship, not that I wanted to know anything about his little wack girlfriend Alexis anyway. From the moment I saw her, I knew she wanted to get back with Randy so it's no surprise they are now dating.

When I made it back to our suite, I found Donovan sitting on the couch typing away on his cell phone.

"Hey baby, I missed you." I said, hoping to get his attention but he continued to be engrossed in his phone. He didn't even blink.

"Whoever you're talking to must be really important for you to ignore me like this." He finally looked up.

"Honey, I'm so sorry. I was talking to one of the pastor's who want to bring me to speak at their conference in Philly soon. I didn't mean to ignore you. I was just trying to hurry up and wrap it up with him. Come here."

Like a little school girl, I sat on his lap. This man had the ability to make me feel like I was sixteen again crushing on the first boy I claimed to love.

"Do you know how excited I am to make you my wife?" Donovan smiled and then stroked the side of my face. Just his mere touch caused me to shiver.

"Tell me again." I held his face in my hands and kissed him softly on the lips. I kept my face close to his and inhaled his scent. He always smelled so good. His cologne danced in and out my nostrils. I closed my eyes and enjoyed every second of it.

"Denise, I can't wait until we are husband and

wife. Now get dressed because I would like to take you on a personal tour of the hotel. It's not like we will be seeing much of it anyway after tomorrow." He winked at me and I took that as my cue to get myself together.

I went in my suitcase and pulled out a sexy royal blue maxi dress that fell to the floor and hit my body in all of the right places. As I got dressed, I overheard Donovan talking to someone on the phone. I couldn't exactly hear what he said since his voice was low. I don't know who he was talking to but, whoever it was, he sounded like they were arguing.

When I came out of the bathroom, he was off the phone but he appeared in deep thought about something.

"Hey baby, what's wrong?"

"Oh nothing. I'm fine babe. I'm just trying to figure out how in the world I'm going to keep my hands off of you until tomorrow." He smiled. I could tell he tried to steer clear of discussing whatever weighed so heavy on his mind.

"I don't know what you're gonna do but whatever it is it must include some prayer and fasting." I laughed.

"In that case, I need to get on my knees right now." He laughed too. Donovan walked over to his suitcase and pulled out a rectangular, gift wrapped box.

"I almost forgot to give you this." I sat on the arm of the couch so that I could open it. I tore the wrapping paper open and saw a brand new pair of Tom Ford shades.

"Baby, these are beautiful. Thank you. You know exactly what I like."

"Anything for you, sweetheart. Glad you like them."

"These are the exact pair I've been looking at for a while now."

"Now we're ready to go on our tour." He grabbed me by my hand and we left our room.

The lobby was full of people. That wasn't surprising at all. Vegas already was a sought after vacation destination but even more at the beginning of June. The Bellagio had so many areas to explore and Donovan was on a mission to show me it all.

"This hotel is so beautiful. I've always seen pictures on the internet but they definitely don't do it any justice." I replied as we walked hand in hand. It wasn't until we were getting ready to walk past the *Petrossian Bar* that I stopped in my tracks.

"Baby, you see that guy over there? He looks just like Malcom." I pointed to the gentleman sitting by himself at the bar, tossing a drink back.

"Who are you talking about?" Donovan asked and tried to keep walking. I stopped and stood there until he came back to me.

"That guy over there looks just like your assistant Malcom." I said and he tried to shrug off my comment until the man at the bar turned around and we made eye contact. As soon as that happened, the man got up from his seat and started walking closer to us. We both realized that it was in fact Malcom.

"Hey Malcom, what are you doing here? I didn't

think we would run into anyone that we knew this weekend." Donovan said as he pressed his jaw together tightly, suggesting to me that he was irritated about something.

"You know what? I was thinking the same exact thing but in Vegas anything is bound to happen. I'm actually here to visit some of my family this weekend. I thought I remember telling you when I asked for time off."

"No, I don't remember that conversation at all."

"Well, I'm surprised to see two. If I didn't know any better, I would think you two were going to get married. You know this is the mecca for elopements."

"Not necessarily though. Denise and I just wanted to get away for the weekend since I have a heavy travel schedule coming up."

"Oh well, you never know because love is truly in the air. My cousin is calling me right now and I have to take this call. You two enjoy yourselves. See you soon." Malcom then walked toward the front of the hotel.

"Wow that was definitely a surprise."

"I'm surprised too. I remember him saying he was taking some time off but I definitely don't remember him telling me he was coming out here."

"Babe, why didn't you just tell him we were getting married? He's going to find out any way."

"I didn't tell him because I wanted to keep this time an intimate moment between us. With my life being so out in the open I have to share everything with the world. Everybody doesn't need to know our personal business.

They will find out in due time."

"Do you think he'll tell anyone?"

"No I doubt it." Donovan replied.

"I don't know if it was just me but did it seem like he was acting a little strange to you?" I asked. Donovan shook his head *no*.

"No. It just looked like Malcom was a little buzzed. That's all."

I started to laugh.

"I didn't know Malcom drank alcohol."

"Oh I've known him to toss back a few from time to time. I don't think he was acting funny. If I were you I wouldn't take anything personal." Donovan reassured me. I don't know if it was just me, but, Malcom just seemed to be a little more antsy than usual. As Donovan's assistant, he was known for always doing a million things at once but he appeared like he was nervous about something.

"Okay honey if you say so." I replied.

"Now if you're ready, I want to show you the chapel we're getting married in tomorrow." Donovan said, ignoring my comment. I didn't make a big deal of it. Instead, we started to resume our tour. Everything else at this point became irrelevant since I was getting ready to become Mrs. Donovan Rodgers.

Chapter 3

Terri

❝You look absolutely breathtaking Denise." I said as I helped my best friend step into her wedding gown and zipped it up for her. The white strapless stretch satin mermaid dress fit her perfectly and made her look much more like a runway model than an actual bride.

"I'm glad you like it Terri. I was nervous when I first decided on this dress but, after I tried it on at my final fitting, I was convinced." Denise smiled.

"You're right about that. You look amazing."

"Thank you for coming here to help me get ready."

"Girl, I wouldn't miss this moment for the world. You were there for me when I had my big day so I wouldn't have it any other way."

I married Carlos last year and Denise stepped in and supported me in a major way. It must've been hard for her since she was in the middle of her divorce but she was still there for me. The way she helped me was something that I would always be grateful for.

"I wonder how the guys are holding up down in your room?" Denise asked as she sat down in a chair for the makeup artist to touch her up.

"Oh I just got off the phone with Carlos. They're fine. They're actually watching ESPN talking about sports." I giggled and Denise started to laugh right along with me.

She shook her head and replied, "That's a man for you."

"I swear, men have it so easy sometimes. All they have to do is get dressed and literally show up. We're the ones that need to labor and sweat to look halfway decent."

"I know that's right. Thanks to my wonderful glam squad they are keeping me together."

"You are already beautiful but they do have you looking like a million bucks."

"That they do." Denise agreed. The hairstylist gave my best friend a multi-layered bob with honey blonde highlights. Honestly, she looked like she just got finished posing for the cover of a magazine. I continued watching them style her to perfection until I received a text from my husband telling us to come down to the chapel.

"Denise." I smiled.

"Yes."

"It's time."

She closed her eyes, took a deep breath, exhaled and then said, "Okay, I'm ready."

We got on the elevator, took it down to the lobby and made our way to the chapel. Denise turned heads the entire way. Everyone kept commenting on how beautiful she looked. I was so happy for her. She had been through so much I'm glad God blessed her with the opportunity to smile again.

The minute the chapel doors opened, our mouths dropped to the floor. Flowers draped the entire room. There were all kind of arrangements and exotic flora lining the aisle. Donovan and Carlos stood at the altar with the minister. From the moment Donovan saw her, he whispered "Wow."

The wedding coordinator handed us both our bouquets. I left Denise to walk down the center aisle and took my place at the altar. I stood opposite my husband then Donovan signaled the coordinator who started playing, *The One He Kept For Me* by Maurette Brown Clark. As my best friend started walking down the aisle, I couldn't do anything but cry. I couldn't even compose myself enough to cry cute. I probably looked a complete mess but I didn't care. It was all pure love for my best friend. She looked so amazing and I was overjoyed to share this special day with her. I looked over at Donovan. His face appeared just as wet as mine. With that, I felt within my heart that my best friend found the right person. I didn't think she would ever find someone who could even compare to Randy but I truly ate my words as I heard her say "I do."

***

"The wedding was so beautiful wasn't it?" I asked Carlos as we got off the elevator and made our way down the hall to our room.

"Yes it was," He replied as he opened our door. The minute I heard our door shut, I turned my back to him so he could unzip my dress. We were going to dinner with the newlyweds but had some time to spare before meeting them.

"It was simple, intimate, and straight to the point."

"Yes, it was nice."

"I really like Donovan for her. He's a good fit for her, don't you think?" I asked.

Carlos paused for a moment and then said, "Uh yeah, I think he's a good fit for her but I don't really know him like that, babe. It's hard for me to make that type of statement and I just met the man today. He seems kind of different though."

"What do you mean?"

"I don't know. It's hard to put my finger on it. I just know it's something."

"Well he had to do or say something for you to have this opinion."

"I don't really know how to explain it. His vibe sort of struck me as odd. That's all," Carlos explained.

"Okay, if you say so. Since he is now married to my best friend, we will definitely get a chance to know him better and I'm sure that you won't feel that way after we spend some time with him."

Carlos held up his phone which interrupted my thoughts. "Look who's calling me." Carlos handed me the phone. When I saw Estella's number flashing across the screen, I rolled my eyes. She always knew how to interrupt a good time.

"Are you going to answer it?" I asked.

"Nope. Estella has the tendency to be the ultimate mood killer and I'm not trying to waste any energy on her foolishness." Carlos pressed ignore on his phone and set it down on the coffee table. It buzzed the minute he released it.

"Babe, she just sent me a text. You have to hear this. She is ridiculous." He read the message aloud.

If you think I'm gonna let our daughter come and be around you and that bitch then you have another thing coming. It will be a cold day in hell before you ever see your daughter again and I mean that...

I rolled my eyes, again. I wished phones possessed an app that would allow me to teleport through it and choke the hell out of her. His ex-wife could be so childish sometimes. Now she knows we planned to come and get Lily all year and wants to pull this stupid stunt right before we come? I know one thing, she was dealing with the wrong one if she thought we were going to stand for such behavior. I couldn't wait to see her face to face. I definitely had a few things I wanted to say to her.

***

We met Donovan and Denise at Twist, a lovely

restaurant inside the Mandarin Oriental Hotel. It was such a beautiful place with an even more romantic ambiance. He reserved a private dining room. The view, as the sun started to set, was absolutely a sight to see.

"Donovan thanks for setting this dinner up. This is a beautiful place." I said.

"You're welcome. It's actually my first time here as well. I'm just as excited as you are. I always wanted to come here when I'm in town and never got the chance." Donovan smiled then kissed my best friend on the lips.

"Please get a room," I said, teasing.

"You're forgetting, we have one." Denise rolled her eyes.

"Yes and we almost didn't make it out on time." Donovan winked at her and I acted as though I got sick to my stomach.

"You two almost got stood up." Denise winked back at her husband. A tall, thin waitress took our drink orders and when she came back to the table, she struck up a conversation.

"Hey, you look so familiar," she said as she passed out our individual drinks.

"Do I?" Donovan asked as he looked at her strangely.

"Yes, you look so familiar like I've seen you before. I'm trying to figure out where I know you from."

"I'm on television quite a lot. Maybe that's where you've seen me." Donovan reassured the waitress. She snapped her fingers as if a light bulb went off in her head.

"I know where I know you from! You always come

in here when you're in town right? You and that other guy that's always with you."

"Oh you must be talking about, Malcom. Yes, he's my assistant and we do frequent this establishment when we're here."

"Ok, well it's a small world and even though Vegas constantly changes I never forget people like you're friend, Malcom. He's someone I would never forget. If you need anything else just call me." She politely smiled and then disappeared off into the kitchen.

"She was surely excited to see you, Donovan." I said. He smiled, slightly.

"I don't think she was excited to see me. She probably thought Malcom was with me. He flirts with that girl big time every time we see her. And he tips her big too, trying to impress her." Donovan laughed.

Denise turned to him and said, "I heard that waitress say that you come here all the time when you're in town. I thought you told me that you had never been here before." Denise raised both of her eyebrows.

"Naw babe, I didn't say I've never been here. I said it's been so long since I've come here it feels like I've never been here." Even though my best friend still looked a bit confused, she shrugged it off and took a sip of her virgin pina colada. I recalled him saying he had never been here too but decided not to butt in.

"Well regardless if this is your first time or not, this girl right here is hungry and I cannot wait to eat. Since this morning, I've worked up quite an appetite if you know what I mean," Denise said and the whole table erupted into laughter.

"If you will excuse me, I have to use the ladies room." I got up from the table.

"I'm coming with you. Baby, we'll be right back." Denise leaned over and gave her new husband a kiss and we walked together.

"Girl, this is so much fun being together in Vegas. This really feels like old times when you and I used to take trips together. But now the only difference is we're both married women now." I said once we walked into the bathroom. Thankfully, I didn't have to wait to use the stall but the stench coming from the restroom made me want to use it as fast as possible so we could get back to our men.

"I don't mean to change the subject but didn't you hear Donovan say that he had never been here before? And that waitress clearly recognized him."

I scrunched my face together. I knew that I heard him clearly.

"Denise, I wasn't going to butt in when we were talking out there but you know I never miss details. I heard him say he had never been to this place before."

"Ok so I'm not the only one that heard him say that. Did I just marry a liar?" Denise asked me.

"You can't be serious, Denise. I don't think he was intentionally lying to you. Maybe he's just excited. I mean he just got married for the first time. You have to put yourself in his shoes. If it was your first time ever being married you would probably be saying wrong stuff too. If I were you I wouldn't worry too much about it." I hoped I was right.

"Okay girl, you're right."

Just then, my phone started to vibrate. I opened my inbox to find that I had a message from Randy. "You will never guess who just text me?"

"You know I'm horrible at guessing so who is it?"

"Randy just sent me a text and asked is it true that you just got married? Apparently, he just saw it on my facebook page. I posted pictures after your ceremony this morning. He didn't know you were getting married?"

"Nope. I told you I didn't tell him."

"So you mean to tell me that he came to get Kaylah and everything and you never mentioned a word of your plans to him?"

"Should I have to? Randy doesn't have to know my every move. Go ahead and answer him. Matter of fact, send him a picture from this morning so he can have a souvenir." Denise crossed her arms.

"No I'm not going to do that. I replied with a yes. I don't know what else to say other than that."

"That's fine. Now if you are done, I would like to get back to my husband." Denise said and we left the bathroom. My best friend always had a way of handling situations. I hoped she chose to deal with her new husband better than she dealt with Randy. If not then she was in for a world of trouble. Because if he wanted to lie about something as small as being at a restaurant, he would lie about anything.

Chapter 4

Randy

I sat at my desk in my office at the church and stared at my Facebook page as I received the shock of my life. Denise got married! The minute I logged into my profile, I saw a post from Terri, a picture of Denise and Minister Donovan Rodgers. People from all over the world congratulated them. Even though Denise and I were friends on Facebook, I didn't make it a habit to snoop on her page. But after seeing this, I decided to click on her profile and check her out. She didn't post anything about the wedding personally but, because Terri tagged her as well as her new husband, her page was already flooded with well wishes from people all across the country. Deacon Russell came in my office as I scrolled back up to the top of the page.

"Hey pastor what's going on?" Deacon asked as he

walked in without knocking or announcing his presence. He was the only person, beside Alexis, who could do that.

"Come here and take a look at this." I let out a chuckle. Deacon came over, took one look at the picture of Denise and started laughing too.

"Denise doesn't waste any time, do she?"

"Apparently not. You know who her new husband is right?"

At first, Russell shook his head no. But, after he took a second look, a light bulb went off in his head.

"Wait a minute. Is that the preacher always on the Light Network?"

"Yes it is," I answered.

"Wow, how in the world did she manage to work that out?"

I shrugged my shoulders.

"Did you even know she was getting married again?"

"Nope. Not at all."

"What did she think, that you would never find out?"

"Your guess is as good as mine. You know Denise always seems to be at the right place and right time. Her making this move doesn't surprise me at all."

I guess I'm surprised because I didn't know she was dating anyone at all. Every time we talked, she made it seem as though her world is all about Kaylah and she doesn't have time for anything else. But now I see that was just a cover-up for what was really going on. I can't be mad at her because I've been dating Alexis seriously but, at least, I waited until we were officially divorced. We barely been divorced for a year and some change and she's already a married woman again. I should be at the point where nothing she does phases me, but sometimes she still had the ability to shock me.

"Well regardless of how you feel about Denise being married at least you can take that as your cue and move on yourself."

I shook my head in agreement with Russell. "I guess you're right about that, Deacon. I have moved on."

"Speaking of moving on, how are you and Alexis doing?"

I smiled when he mentioned her name. "We are actually great. We have a date tonight. I'm taking her to Pittsburgh so we can check out the Savoy."

"Oh, that's a nice place there. I took Sheila there a few months ago for our anniversary."

"For real? I didn't know you had already been there."

"Randy, it's a lot of things you don't know about me. When it comes to romance, I am the master. Don't let this old age fool you." Russell started popping his collar. I acted like I was completely grossed out and covered my ears.

"Okay, stop right there. That's too much information. I don't wanna know anything else."

"Okay Randy, you can stop me if you want to but

I'm telling you. You could learn a few things from me."

"Yeah I guess." I laughed.

"Well, I think that's nice you're taking her out. Alexis is a nice woman. A lot nicer than Genevieve." Russell snickered. He lived to bring that woman's name up.

At the mention of her name, I started to shutter right there in my seat. I rolled my eyes at Russell because he always blew that situation up. When Denise and I were first going through our divorce, we tried our best to maintain our privacy. But with thousands of members at Oakdale Baptist, the news of our separation and subsequent divorce spread like wildfire. I went from no attention to every available woman in my church and every other church in my face. From the attention I received from my female parishioners, you would've thought I was a famous rapper or an athlete. My private, unlisted cell number turned into a hotline. There were countless visits from women who offered to cook for me because they felt that no man of God should starve. I did pretty well with fighting off the masses but there was always one who managed to slip through the cracks, including Genevieve Albright. Genevieve was what I liked to call a seasoned woman, at least fifteen years my senior. But she aged gracefully. She had the body of a twenty year old, and sad to say, the mentality to match. Once she set her sights out on me, she pursued me with everything in her. She would stop by my office and my house unannounced and, when that didn't work, she resorted to desperate measures. She forced me to put my foot down when she mailed me a pair of her underwear claiming, *there's more where that came from.*

Rumor has it, she has slept with quite a few men in my congregation. And, if that wasn't bad enough, she had her greedy little paws out for me. When Deacon Russell got wind of Genevieve trying to make passes at me, he wouldn't let me live it down.

"Why must you bring her up every chance you get?" I asked. He started to laugh uncontrollably. I'm glad he at least finds this funny. Deacon Russell's infectious laugh caused me to break down and laugh with him.

"Because Genevieve wanted you so bad. She could literally be your mother. You know she tried to come at me a few times but Sheila dealt with her right on the spot, and that was that. On the other hand, I heard she isn't anything to play with in the bedroom."

"And those diseases she probably has aren't anything to play with either. Russell, I'm not thinking about Genevieve." I started laughing all over again. Leave it up to him to say some crazy off the wall stuff to me. He was like that crazy uncle who always embarrassed everybody at the family gatherings.

"All jokes aside, I really do think Alexis is a nice young woman for you and I can't wait until you two make it official."

"One day, Deacon. It will happen."

"Who's watching Kaylah while you and Alexis go out? You're more than welcome to drop her by the house. Sheila and I would love to spend some time with her."

"Well I will definitely take you up on that offer. I

will call you before we come."

I could see myself marrying Alexis but wasn't in a rush. I wanted to take my time and make sure we did everything right. After Russell left my office, I sent Denise a text. I didn't mention the fact that I knew she had gotten married.

Hey Denise I know you've probably been busy but when you get a moment please call me I would like to talk to you about something.

The fast response I received from Denise you would've probably thought Jesus himself was texting her because in less than thirty seconds I already had a response.

About what?

Nothing major, just wanted to take Kaylah on a shopping spree and buy her some things before I bring her back home and need some insight on the sizes she wears. That's all.

Ok...cool. Are you sure that's the only reason why you text me?

Yes. Why would you ask that?

I dunno what she wanted just seemed a little random to me. That's all.

I promise you that's all I wanted. Didn't mean to disturb you. I will make sure Kay calls you before she goes to bed tonight.

I replied and smiled because she probably thought I had actually texted her to ask her about her so called marriage. I mentioned nothing about that and I knew it bothered her because she knew that I had to know something.

Oh okay, well I will call you soon…

Traffic seemed to be extra heavy on the Pennsylvania Turnpike as we made our way to the Savoy. The weekend proved to be the time where everyone sought to be entertained in Pittsburgh. Thank God we left early enough in advance so we could at least make it to the restaurant on time. We pulled up just in time. I dropped Alexis off at the entrance then I parked my car. When I came through the door, she had the biggest smile on her face.

"This place is so nice. I love the way they've decorated it. It's so romantic."

"It is. I'm glad you like it. Deacon Russell said we would."

"Yes I love it."

The waitress led us to an exclusive part of the restaurant and seated us in a plush white booth. When Alexis looked down, she smiled as she saw our names written decoratively on a tray with a bouquet of flowers just for her.

"All this for me?" she asked.

"Of course, why not?"

"I dunno, honey. I'm just not used to stuff like this. Teddy was far from the romantic type."

"I bet. Well you can forget Teddy. He's your past and I'm your future and this is how I choose to do things."

"And what a beautiful future it is." She winked at me. Since Alexis and I had been dating, she had been nothing short of a blessing. It tickled me to think I had reconnected with my first love. She would've actually been my wife first but everything happens for a reason and, without being married to Denise, I would've never been blessed with the opportunity to be a father to Kaylah. Even though she was not my biological daughter I still considered it a great privilege to be the father in her life. And being married Denise taught me a valuable lesson. It taught me about the type of woman that I didn't want to be with. Most would call my relationship with Denise a complete waste of time but I didn't see it that way. It was a life lesson that I am forever grateful for. If I had never been married to Denise, I would never be able to appreciate a woman like Alexis coming into my life.

"Babe you'll never guess what I found out today."

"What?"

"Denise got married again to some TV preacher."

"For real? Wow!"

"I was shocked too. I didn't even know she was dating."

"Denise is known for making some sneaky moves when it comes to things in her life. I'm just glad she will finally leave you alone. To me, its closure and we can finally move forward together."

"You're right. I didn't look at it that way."

Alexis made a very good point. With Denise finally being someone's wife it made her someone else's problem and it gave me the freedom to move on with my life too. And I planned on doing just that.

Chapter 5

Denise

The church folks at Deliverance Ministries International already didn't like me as Donovan's girlfriend so, the minute I became a permanent fixture in his life, their disdain for me escalated to an entirely different level. The way those women acted toward me, you would've thought I married Lebron James or Jay-Z.

Donovan pulled our Bentley Continental GT in our reserved parking space, situated right next to the pastor and our first lady. I observed a handful of women standing not too far from our car, having a conversation. The minute they saw us, their faces twisted up so tight that they all appeared distorted. I still managed to smile even though I honestly felt like doing the opposite. My natural reaction was to mean mug the hell out of them but that wouldn't have been Christian like of me.

When I stepped out of the car, they stopped talking. The silence became so great that you could hear a pin drop right there in the parking lot. So instead of allowing the silence to continue, I did what I felt was proper since all eyes were on me anyway. I opened up my mouth and spoke.

"Good morning ladies! It's such a beautiful day to come into the house of the Lord." I smiled and gave them a good glimpse of my wedding ring for good measure. I reached in the back seat and helped my daughter get out of the car. As soon as her feet hit the ground, she ran around the car and grabbed Donovan's hand. The entire group of women looked like they were utterly disgusted by how I handled the situation. I smiled. I didn't care. I slightly adjusted my navy blue Tracy Reese dress then walked over to my husband and kissed him on the cheek. We all walked hand in hand into the church.

"Those ladies were happy to see us this morning," Donovan said with a grin on his face.

"They sure were." I snickered underneath my breath.

Beautiful cherry wood pews lined the five thousand seat sanctuary from wall to wall. They provided perfect accent to the royal purple carpet extending the entire length of the massive room. Every time I walked into this space, I felt invincible. I felt like I could conquer the world and it even felt more amazing to be married to a man involved with one of the most powerful ministries in the world.

Strutting down the center aisle of the sanctuary felt like being in the middle of a runway show during fashion week. If you were brave enough to walk down the center, you better give the people something fierce to look at. Believe me, I didn't disappoint. I gave those women something fashionable to look at for the last four months. I knew they probably had to be pulling out their phones to sneak and take pictures of what I had on. Shoot, if I were in their position, I would take pictures of me too.

I usually sat near the front of the sanctuary with Donovan's mother Joann and Shay, Donovan's secretary. My husband always sat in the pulpit with the various clergy members and this Sunday was no different. I had to admit it felt good to be married to a man in the spotlight once again.

"Denise, you look so nice," Shay whispered. I responded with a simple, "Thanks girl." Out of all the people I've encountered since my move to Florida, she's been the nicest, most genuine person that I've come across. Shay Klucher had to be one of the coolest down to earth women that I've met. Her maturity, for her age, surprised me. Shay's intuitive mind and charm made her the perfect person to assist my husband in the day to day operations of his ministry.

Midway through worship service, I had to use the restroom. I wanted to use it before the sermon. Because there wasn't anything tackier than excusing yourself while the pastor preached.

"Can you keep an eye on Kaylah while I go to the bathroom," I asked Shay.

"Of course," she answered. I got up and walked down the outer aisle toward the direction of Donovan's office. I was so glad my husband had enough clout and position to afford him his own personal office and bathroom because I despised using public restrooms.

When I walked into Donovan's office, I saw Malcom sitting at Donovan's desk, engrossed in a telephone conversation. I smiled and waved at him and, without even looking up, he sort of waved me away and continued on with his conversation. Without responding to him, I walked pass him and went to the bathroom. At first glance, it seemed like he had an attitude when he saw me but I wanted to give him the benefit of the doubt because I didn't know him too well.

By the time I came out, he had ended the call. I decided to break the ice with a compliment.

"You're looking good today, Malcom." I smiled and took a good look at his outfit. I briefly had a chance to check out his outfit when we first arrived at church. But, after an up close and personal look, I was truly impressed. His tailored-made suit fit him perfectly and the lavender tie he wore around his neck was an identical match with his lavender dress socks. Even though I didn't truly know him that well, I knew that he was extremely meticulous about his looks. He kept a low cut fade with a crisp line up and his hands stayed with a fresh manicure. He had to be the most stylish man I had ever met. Even his so-called raggedy clothes were all designer as Malcom made it a point to wear nothing but the best.

Malcom pressed his lips together and offered me a tight smile. I guess he considered that as an acknowledgement of my comment. Whatever he determined it to be, it still seemed like he had an attitude.

"Denise, I didn't mean to be short with you when you first walked in. I was working on an event your husband is supposed to be doing in Atlanta soon and was trying to make sure everything is on point."

I held up my hands. "It's fine Malcom. I understand."

"Well if you'll excuse me I need to hop on the phone again."

"Don't worry. I was just leaving."

I don't know if it was just me but it seemed like every time I saw Malcom he acted like he didn't want to be bothered. Since he was the closest person to my husband besides me I really wanted to develop a closer relationship with him. He knew Donovan better than anyone. It seemed as though he only tolerated me.

I walked down the long hallway and, once I got to the lobby, I saw that same group of haters standing around in a circle talking. Obviously, they were talking about me. They kept whispering and looking over at me like I couldn't figure out what they saying. I made sure I looked over at them, rolled my eyes and walked away with an extra strut in my step. As far as I was concerned, none of those homely looking women could hold a candle to me even on my worst day so I gave them the same attitude they gave me. It ate them up and there was nothing more satisfying than seeing them squirm. I walked back into the sanctuary just in time to hear the pastor's opening scripture.

When the service ended, we usually hung around the sanctuary for a little while Donovan greeted members with the pastor. I sat on the front pew and patiently waited for him to be done. Donovan gave his pastor a hug and then walked down the steps to where Kaylah and I were sitting.

"Hey love are you ready to get out of here?"

"Absolutely."

When we were walking back to the car, Donovan informed me that he'd already made reservations for dinner and I wasn't complaining about that since I wouldn't have to cook Sunday Dinner. We pulled up to *Norman's* at The Ritz-Carlton and ended up with a table out on the terrace.

"This is a beautiful view, sweetheart." I said taking in a view of the lake and the golf course that was close by.

"Not more beautiful than you. I wanted us to have a nice dinner together as a family. Especially since Kaylah just came back from being in Ohio with her daddy."

"This was nice of you. Kaylah and I really appreciate this."

"Of course. Princess did you have fun when you were with your daddy?"

"Yes, my daddy took me everywhere. And I went over Ms. Alexis house too. I had fun." Kaylah smiled.

"Well you know what? I am so glad that you had fun but I'm happy that you are back with us. And I have a surprise for you princess." Donovan revealed and Kaylah's eyes grew big. I was surprised too because he never told me that he was planning any surprise for her.

"I have a surprise?" Kaylah asked practically

jumping out of her chair. She was definitely her mother's child. I loved surprises and receiving gifts.

Donovan reached in his suit jacket and pulled out a box. He opened it up and then turned the box around for her to see.

"I got you a necklace that says Papa's girl. You are my special princess and I promise to always take care of you and be there for you. I love you lil mama." He replied and then removed the necklace and put it around her neck.

"Thanks Papa!" She jumped up and wrapped her arms around his neck the minute he finished putting the jewelry on her.

"Baby, this is such a great thing for you to do. I really appreciate it from the bottom of my heart. It takes a special man to raise a child that's not their own so I don't take what you do for her lightly. I love you so much."

"I love you and Kaylah as well. I've always wanted children so having Kaylah in my life is just a great addition. I promise to always do right by you two. I definitely don't take being a husband and father for granted."

The next day Shay and I decided to get together and meet up at the mall. Shay liked to shop just as much as I did. We decided to meet up at the Florida Mall and have lunch together. Since I didn't know too many people in Orlando, it felt good to be able to get a little relaxation time that wasn't church related.

"It feels good to finally be doing what I love to do and that's shop. Thanks for meeting me," I said as I sat across from Shay at the California Pizza Kitchen.

"Thanks for inviting me. You know I love a good excuse to get a little retail therapy in," Shay replied.

"I know that's right and I am long overdue." With Donovan in meetings all day, I sent Kaylah to daycare and decided I would take some time to myself.

"I am so glad Donovan chose you as his wife. For a while, I was worried."

"Worried about what?"

"Girl, I was worried that he was never going to find him a wife and get married. For a minute, all he was focused on was travelling the country with Malcom and speaking. Just glad he's taking the time to really live his life." Shay smiled and I did too.

"Well, I'm glad you like me."

"Of course, you're one of the coolest women I've met in a long time and your daughter is absolutely gorgeous."

"Why thank you."

Shay's cell phone began to ring. She paused to answer it.

"Hey, what's up? Oh you're at the mall shopping. Well, guess what, I'm here too. I'm at California Pizza Kitchen. Okay. See ya in a few. Alright bye." Shay hung up the phone and placed it back inside her mint Michael Kors purse.

"Who was that?"

"Oh, that was Malcom. He's out here shopping too so he's about to meet us for lunch." And before I even had a chance to respond, he walked toward our table.

"Hello." Malcom waved and stood closest to Shay.

"I should've known you were gonna be out here shopping. You shop more than me," Shay said as he draped his bags in the chair next to her.

"From the looks of it, you've done some major damage," I added as I looked over at all of his bags. He had more than I could count.

"No, not really. I didn't know you were out here with Shay. To be honest, I didn't think a high end mall was your style. Anyways, Shay you could've told me y'all were having a girl's day then I would've caught up with you later," Malcom said almost as fast as he blinked. I sat there on pause, trying to figure out if he implied that I wear cheap clothes? I didn't know whether to be offended or just laugh.

"Malcom, it's not a problem at all. Actually, if you would like, you can feel free to join us," Shay offered.

Malcom glanced down at his platinum Rolex watch and replied, "Oh, no thank you. Besides, I have somewhere to be in like an hour anyway." If his reply was any dryer, I would have been able to bottle it up and sell it as starch.

"Well excuse me."

"Oh, I almost forgot to tell you. Guess what I just brought?" Malcom looked briefly at Shay.

"What?"

"Those Gucci sneakers I've been eyeing for the

last month."

"I knew it! I knew you were gonna break down and get them."

"Baby listen. You know Malcom got to stay fresh. Any fresher and I would be an infant." He smiled and then cockily popped his collar.

"You are crazy." Shay laughed, then got up from the table and gave him a hug.

"Okay call me later."

"Bye girl." He walked away.

"Bye Malcom," I said, still trying to be cordial.

"Mmmmhmmm." Malcom mumbled and then left the restaurant. I watched him walk away and couldn't do anything but laugh.

"Your boy Malcom is something else." I shook my head back and forth.

"What do you mean?"

"Shay, this is the second time he's brushed me off. The first time was at church right after we got back from Vegas and just now. You don't see him acting funny toward me?"

"No I don't think he was acting funny. Maybe you two need to get used to each other. That's all. If I were you, I wouldn't worry about it."

"Really?"

"Yeah, when I first started being around Malcom, I thought the same thing. So don't worry about it. In time, you'll see. Things will change."

Even though I wanted to believe her, I had a feeling this was just the way it was going to be between him and I.

After I left the mall with Shay, I pulled out my phone and called my husband. With Kaylah still being at daycare, I figured it would be nice to have a little alone time before picking her up. His phone went straight to voicemail. Instead of trying to call him again, I just ended up driving home.

When I got there, Donovan still wasn't there and I wasn't expecting him since he had multiple meetings. I figured I would sit in our entertainment room and catch up on all the reality shows I've missed since I'd gotten married. Thank God for DVR. I was in the middle of catching up on an episode of "Basketball Wives LA" when my phone started ringing. I smiled when I saw Donovan's name on the screen. I answered his call and, when I said hello, all I heard was noise in the background. I was getting ready to hang up, thinking he called me by mistake when I heard a voice say, "I love you baby, I've missed you so much. I'm just glad we got to spend some time together."

"Me too. I'm glad we got a chance to be together today," Another voice replied. The voices sounded muffled so it was hard to make out who they belonged to. I felt safe to assume that one of them were Donovan's. I tried to continue to listen to the conversation but the phone call ended. I was completely furious and couldn't wait until he got home because believe me as God as my witness there will be hell to pay.

"So where were you?" I asked the minute Donovan stepped foot through the door.

"Oh, I just got done with my last meeting of the day. I'm glad to finally be home," Donovan replied and then sat his briefcase down near the bottom of the steps.

"So you just left a meeting huh? At two in the morning? That's the truth? You just left a meeting? Notice I keep asking you over and over the same question. I'm giving you ample opportunity to tell the truth before I go the hell off."

"First of all, Denise, why are you cussing at me? And why are you even upset in the first place?"

"Answer the question, Donovan. Where did you just come from?"

The more he delayed an answer, the angrier I became. I literally felt like my entire body was on fire.

"Like I told you before, Denise, I just came from my last meeting. I'm still trying to understand what has you so upset."

"Okay since you're trying to play like you have amnesia or something, let me lay it all out for you. When I got home from the mall, I called you but my call went straight to voicemail. A few hours later, you ended up calling me back. I could hear you in the background with some female. She was telling you how she missed you and you were saying the same thing. So does any of this jog your memory? You ready to come clean now?" I crossed my arms over my chest. I felt like it was the best stance to avoid slapping him or throwing something.

"Denise, you sound absolutely crazy right now. First of all, I don't have to confess anything because I haven't done anything. I was exactly where I said I was... at a meeting. You think I'm cheating on you?" he asked.

"You tell me. Your phone is the one that called me. I'm not making this stuff up. You called me."

"I'm telling you that wasn't me at all. I was in a meeting with a bunch of elders. I wasn't spending time with some woman. Maybe my phone call to you was intercepted. It happens all the time."

"What are you talking about?"

"I'm not denying the fact that I did call you. I am denying that it was me on the other end. My phone line had to be intercepted."

"Your phone line was intercepted? Come on, Donovan. Do you honestly think I was born yesterday? Just admit that it was you."

"No because that wasn't me. Do you think I would've married you, if I was going to be out here cheating on you? That's not me at all, Denise. What I can't seem to understand is how you're so quick to assume that I'm out here doing wrong. Where's your trust at? If we're going to be married then you're going to have to trust me." He explained and then pulled out his cell phone right in front of me.

"What are you doing? I asked. He handed me the phone.

"I've unlocked my phone and you are more than welcome to look through everything. And you will see that I'm telling you the truth." Donovan started to walk away.

"Where are you going?"

"I'm going upstairs to take a shower and go to bed."

He left me completely speechless. I didn't know whether to be pissed off or take him up on his offer to play Inspector Gadget. You know what I chose to do right? I went through the phone! I went through every text message, every picture, every download, and every email. After that, I was right back where I started. I had nothing. I felt like a complete idiot thinking I was getting ready to open pandora's box and I didn't find anything. Finally, I went up the steps and joined my husband in bed. He slept so peacefully as if he didn't have a care in the world. I was the one who had the weight of the world on my shoulders and couldn't exactly put my finger on a reason why. Any other woman would've been in heaven to have complete access to their husband's phone. They would've been even more relieved to have found nothing. However, I on the other hand wasn't pleased in the least bit. I know what I initially heard on the phone. In this moment, I appeared to be nothing more than a paranoid and insecure woman but I wasn't born yesterday. I guess he thought he solved the problem I had with him by giving me his phone, but even though it may have temporarily prevented a blow up between us I knew it was like lava in a volcano waiting to explode at the right moment. I could feel it.

Chapter 6

Terri

"Lily can you come downstairs? It's time to eat!" I announced from the bottom of the steps. I made sure my voice was loud enough to hear me no matter where she was. Assuming she heard me, I walked back to the dining room and continued setting the table. After about five minutes, she hadn't come downstairs. I called her name again. She still didn't respond. I was getting ready to call her name again when Carlos walked through the door.

"Hey love. Where's Lily?" Carlos walked up to me and kissed me on my lips.

"She's upstairs in her room baby. I've been calling her for the last few minutes and she hasn't come down yet."

Carlos walked to the edge of the steps, where I

previously stood and called his daughter's name. Before he could say her name a second time she immediately ran down the steps as if she was a track star.

"Okay daddy." She gave me a funny look.

Did this child just blatantly ignore me?

Throughout the whole course of dinner my mind drifted back and forth to the ordeal we encountered at Estella's house when we went to pick up Lily. We left Vegas the day after Denise got married. Our trip to Estella's house was a true act of faith. She sent multiple text messages while we were in Vegas. The text that took the cake was the one she sent the morning we were leaving to come and get her. She claimed she wasn't sure if she was comfortable letting her child go with someone she didn't know (and that someone being me). Even though Carlos is her father and I'm his wife but that all seemed to be null and void just because I was added to the equation. We made a decision that we would go anyway and at least give it a try. I knew I truly loved Carlos because I really wanted to grab his phone from him and give this heifer a piece of my mind. Out of respect for my husband and how volatile their relationship was already, I decided to play the background on this one.

When our taxi pulled up in front of Estella's tudor style home, I said a silent prayer, that we would be able to take Lily for the summer and I would not get arrested in the process. To our surprise, Estella sat on her wrap around front porch in a rocking chair when we arrived. I told Carlos that we should go and meet her together. I wanted to show her that, not only was I highly capable of caring for my stepdaughter I wasn't afraid of her either. The minute I got out of the taxi, the look on her face changed the moment she saw me. I was dressed to impress and had the biggest smile on my face. My mother always said *"kill 'em with kindness."* Besides you could get more bees with honey anyway. If she wasn't pissed about my sweet disposition, then the Michael Kors Romper and matching sandals sent her over the edge. The designer garment hit every curve on my body like a sports car on an obstacle course. Even my husband had to do a double take when I got dressed that morning.

"Hi Estella, this is my wife Terri. Baby, this is Estella. Where's my baby girl at?" Carlos asked. Estella shifted her eyes from my husband and then shifted all her attention and focus on me.

"Hi Terren. Carlos, your daughter is inside waiting for you."

I smiled when I heard her pronounce my name wrong. I had to remember, I just prayed. That was literally the only thing saving her at this particular moment. Besides, if Estella considered that her "A" game, she would be no match for me at all.

"Is she packed and ready to go?" he asked.

"Of course. Why wouldn't she be?" She responded.

"Need I remind you of all the recent text messages you've been sending me."

"Come on, please. I know we've had our issues in the past but you don't think I would be that petty and play games, now would you?"

I didn't mean to judge but was this chick bipolar or something? This was the same woman who sent him all kinds of nasty text messages and who had him locked up before we were married. Now all of a sudden, she's incapable of doing childish stuff? She wasn't fooling anyone but herself.

"You really don't want me to answer that question. I'm going to go in and get my daughter so we can all make our flight in time." Carlos opened up the screen door and walked in the house, leaving me and this little evil wench alone.

As soon as Carlos shut the door behind him, Estella took that as her cue to get real.

"Hmm… so you're the one Carlos married, huh?"

I didn't respond. I just looked at her.

"I hope you cherish all this while it lasts. Because from the looks of you, it won't last long. And…"

"Stop right there. Just because I'm quiet doesn't mean I'm weak. I have a vocabulary and a way with words that will make your head spin. You may not like that Carlos and I are together, but let's get something straight. I am his wife. Not his girlfriend, some groupie, or hoe. His wife. Which means what we have is forever. You may not even want to accept it but it is reality. The real problem is your daughter is caught in the middle of all this. I will not be going back and forth with you like we are some wanna be reality show divas. We will come at each other with respect or not at all. You may not like me but you will respect me."

She clapped as if she applauded a performance.

"Oh save your Rosa Parks speech for someone who really cares because I sure don't." She crossed her arms and rolled her eyes. I could tell I got all underneath her skin and that's all I wanted to do. Carlos and Lily came out of the house just as we were about to begin round two and I was thankful.

"Hi Ms. Lily. Do you have everything you need?" I asked her as I took one of her suitcases and gave her a hug.

"Yes, my daddy double checked everything," she replied and I looked over at Estella who tried so hard to compose herself. I laughed underneath my breath because I knew I had her right where I wanted. My many years as a lawyer made me an expert at keeping my cool under pressure. She unfortunately wasn't blessed with that gift.

"Come here baby and give me a hug and a kiss. Mommy's gonna miss you!" Estella said as Lily walked over to her mother and did as asked. She waited until she hugged her to roll her eyes at me. I didn't care. It was fun to finally be able to give her a run for her money in person. She must've thought Carlos new wife would fold under pressure but I definitely had news for her. I was nothing to play with.

"Bye mommy. I love you Lily!" She said, as she made her way to the taxi.

"Nice meeting you, Estella," I said as I waited until everyone got in the vehicle. The look on her face was priceless. That gave me satisfaction alone.

"Babe what do you think about what I just said?" Carlos asked as my attention snapped back into the conversation at our dinner table.

"I'm sorry sweetie, what did you just say?" I asked.

"You've been drifting in and out of the conversation this entire time. You've barely touched your food."

"I know. I'm really not that hungry anyway. Where's Lily?" I asked when I realized she wasn't anywhere in sight.

"She already finished eating dinner. She went back upstairs so she could facetime with some of her friends."

"Oh okay. Babe, I know this is gonna sound silly but I think she was ignoring me earlier."

"You really think she was ignoring you? She know I don't play around when it comes to stuff like that. I don't know, maybe she had her headphones on and didn't hear you."

"I dunno. Maybe you're right."

There was a part of me that truly wanted to believe that it was a misunderstanding and Lily really didn't hear me but I couldn't help but lean more towards Lily purposely not wanting to hear me.

Chapter 7

Denise

"Honey, I think hosting this game night at our house was a great idea," I said as I walked in from the garage, carrying bags of various games.

"Me too. I honestly think this will be a good way for us to all spend time together. We never get that opportunity with me always being on the road."

"I agree. Did our chef prepare everything we requested?"

"Babe he did that and some. He even made that buffalo chicken dip that you love."

"Perfect. Have you talked to everyone? Are they on their way?" I continued as Donovan helped me bring all the stuff into our living room.

"Yes, I talked to Shay and she's already in route. I

couldn't get a hold of Malcom but I did send him a text so he should be coming."

"Okay that sounds great."

"I brought every game I could think of, so we should have a great time."

Ever since Donovan suggested we hold a game night at our home as a way for me to get to know Shay and Malcom, I thought it was such a good idea. I already got along well with Shay but figured it would be a great way for Malcom to warm up to me.

Shay arrived shortly after I started setting the table in the dining room.

"Thanks for coming tonight. We really appreciate it." Shay followed me from the front door to our living room.

"Girl, you know I wouldn't miss this for the world. Any opportunity where we get a chance to do something that isn't work related, I want to take advantage of."

"I feel you." I giggled.

Donovan came down the stairs and hugged Shay. "Shay have you talked to Malcom at all today? Did he tell you he was still coming?" he asked.

"Um, when I talked to him earlier he said that he would still come. I tried to call him while I was driving on my way here and I went straight to his voicemail."

"Okay, well we can relax for a few while we wait on him. Shay, feel free to go into our dining room and help yourself to the food," I announced. We sat and waited another fifteen minutes. I didn't think he would show up.

"Honey, maybe Malcom had something come up. We can go ahead and start without him." Donovan looked at his watch. Then in almost an instant, our doorbell rang again. I went to the door and opened it. "I'm so glad that you could make it, Malcom."

"Well I figured this game night wouldn't be right unless I showed up, so here I am." Malcom hurried past me and into the living room where Donovan and Shay sat.

"Hey Malcom, I'm glad you came. We didn't think you were coming," Donovan said then slapped hands with Malcom. They gave each other a hug.

"I wouldn't miss this game night for the world," he sarcastically replied. I looked over at him and studied his countenance. He looked annoyed as ever be at our house for game night but I wasn't going to let his sarcasm and his attitude ruin this wonderful evening we were going to have.

"I swear you don't have any sense, Malcom. So what game do you all want to play first? I vote for spades," Shay said as she found the deck of cards on the table and started waving them around.

"Shay you know how to play spades?" I asked.

"Girl, I don't know about y'all but they call me a legend around here." Shay said bragging. I couldn't do anything but laugh.

"Okay, spade champion of the world. We can play spades," Donovan said as he took the deck of cards from her.

"Hey how about we play a friendly game of scrabble. I'm feeling like a wordsmith tonight," Malcom suggested.

"Let's play on teams. Denise and I against you two," Shay said. We all agreed. We rolled the dice and determined the guys would go first.

"I'm going to let Malcom represent our team and go first," said Donovan.

"Gladly," he replied and then began to arrange his letters in front of him. When he finished, he had a smirk on his face and then placed his word on the board.

"S-L-U-T. Slut," he said reciting the letters like some kid in the spelling bee.

"I guess you're really trying to win. I can't believe you would spell that word." Shay shook her head at him.

"Why not? In scrabble, I take no prisoners. I use all my blocks no matter what they spell. Now, let's see what you have." Malcom challenged us and I told Shay I already saw a word that we could use. I placed my words on the board and then I spelled it out like he had done.

"I-R-R-E-L-E-V-A-N-T. Irrelevant," I said with the sweetest smile on my face. Out of the corner of my eyes, I could see Malcom rolled his eyes at me. But as far as I was concerned, we were playing an innocent game of scrabble.

"Okay, so I'm going next. You two have spelled some interesting words. Okay, I have one. P-E-A-C-E. Peace." Donovan tried to decrease the tension that seemed thick as smoke in the room.

"Oh, I think you guys will like my word. S-H-A-Y. Shay," Shay said. We all erupted into laughter.

"I'm sorry to inform you but that's definitely not a word." Donovan laughed and Shay took her word off the board.

"Y'all know it's a word. Shoot, it is my name. I quit Scrabble. Let's go and eat and play another game after."

"You know what, I agree. This scrabble game was over before it started anyway." Malcom rolled his eyes and pulled out his cell phone and began looking through it.

"I cannot wait until you all taste what our chef has made us for tonight." I led everyone into the dining room.

"I smell seafood. What did the chef actually make?" Malcom asked with his nose turned up in the air. If his nose were any higher it would be turned upside down.

"Yes, you smell seafood because he made a few seafood dishes per my request. But that's not all he prepared for us tonight. If you're so unhappy with everything, you can leave." I suggested. Everyone in the room turned to where Malcom and I were standing. Their mouths were hanging wide open. I know they weren't expecting me to say that but I felt it needed to be said especially since I had went to great lengths to try and provide a classy and fun night for all of us. He had done nothing but give off bad vibes since he'd walked through the door. I started to ignore him and since I didn't know him that well I tried to give him the benefit of the doubt but I couldn't help myself in this moment.

"I'm not unhappy I'm just saying I'm allergic to

seafood and I thought that was all that was available." Malcom tried to switch up his attitude but it was still evident that he had one.

"Well it doesn't seem that way to me. It seems to me like you didn't want to come in the first place. If that were the case you really didn't have to show up we would've been just fine without you." I stated and then gave him a look that suggested that I wasn't about to go back and forth with him trying to accommodate him when he knew good and well that he was being a complete jerk.

Malcom seemed to be searching for words to say when my husband took that as his opportunity to interject and switch up the direction that our conversation was going.

"Baby, honestly I think there has been some huge misunderstanding between you two. Malcom, is very appreciative of what you've put together for tonight. Aren't you Malcom?" He looked over at Malcom who pressed his lips together tightly and replied, "Yes, Denise I appreciate what you put together. Don't pay me any attention."

"I mean we are all grateful for this beautiful game night. Before you came into the picture we never really had a chance to just kick back and relax. If it was outside of the ministry and work related stuff then it wasn't happening. And with that being said let us all join hands so that I can bless the food."

Donovan stepped in between us and joined hands with Malcom and I so we were separated. Good thing he did because the way I was feeling I would've tried to break his wrist during the prayer. He could try and suddenly appear that he was thankful for game night all he wanted but I could see straight through him like he was some sheer curtains. He wasn't fooling anybody but himself.

Chapter 8

Denise

The minute I pulled up to the church, I noticed Donovan's car wasn't in the parking lot in his usual space. *So much for trying to surprise him.* I knew I should've just called first but one can't blame me for trying to be a bit spontaneous. I walked into Donovan's office and found a post-it note.

***Hey baby, I stopped by to take you out to lunch as a surprise but since you're not here. I'll just surprise you later. I promise it will be worth your while.* ☺**

I stuck the note on his computer screen so, when he sat down, it would be the first thing he saw. I also took another post-it note and kissed it so I could leave him a trace of my lipstick. When I looked up, Malcom was standing in the doorway staring at me as if I had just stolen something.

"Hey Malcom." I smiled even though his vibe seemed far from friendly.

"Denise." He replied, dryly. If his response was any drier, it would've needed some water to revive it. He walked past me and sat some papers down on Donovan's desk. I noticed that he glanced at my handwritten note and then shook his head.

"Malcom, look. I know we don't know each other too well but I've never been one to beat around the bush about anything so I'm just going to say it. Do you have a problem with me? Have I done something to you for you to act the way you do toward me?"

"What would make you think that I don't like you?" He acted totally clueless to his own behavior.

"Come on, Malcom. Let's not do this please. Ever since Donovan first introduced me and you, it seems like you have this attitude with me. And last time I checked, I thought I always treated you with nothing but respect. So I'm giving you an opportunity to speak up now. You can sit here and act like you don't have a clue to what I'm saying to you, but I do know my thoughts are valid." I stated.

"Okay, so you really want to know how I feel? I honestly feel like you came out of nowhere. Like you literally fell out of the sky. One minute Donovan was single and the next he was head over hills supposedly in love with someone he barely even knows."

"Can I ask you a question? Why do you care so much?"

"I care because Donovan is a dear friend to me

and it is my job to have his back and look out for him. Especially when I don't know what your personal motives are toward him."

I held up my finger to pause him. "Wait a minute. My motives? Now you're questioning me and my motives? Since you think God has blessed you with psychic ability and you know me so well, please tell me what my motives supposedly are." I crossed my arms and awaited this response. I couldn't wait to hear what this fool had to say.

"Listen, I don't know what your exact motives are but I can't tell you how many women have come around thinking they were gonna attach themselves to him because of the mere fact he's in the spotlight and he has money and you seem like that type."

I laughed at his response. "Are you serious right now? If you think I married Donovan because of his money, you're sadly mistaken. I definitely didn't marry him for any money. And just so we're clear, I had money and affluence well before I met Donovan. I didn't choose to be with him because of his status. I married him because I love him."

"Hmph. Only time will truly tell." He rolled his eyes.

I shrugged off his snide remark. I had to because, if I didn't, I would be wrapping my hands around his scrawny little neck.

"Listen, you may have a million and one reasons why you don't like me but that's not my concern or what I care about. Just because you don't like me, doesn't throw out the validity of my presence or diminish my position in his life. I'm here to stay and there is nothing you or anyone else can do to change that. You may as well get used to me because I'm definitely a permanent fixture all up and through here."

"Okay we'll see." Malcom gave me the sneakiest smile just as Donovan walked through the door.

"What's going on in here?" Donovan asked as he could see the look on my face. I was absolutely pissed and probably would've cussed Malcom's ass out right then and there but I was trying to turn over a new leaf in my life and maintain my poise and class at all times. But Malcom surely was testing my limits.

"Oh nothing. We're cool. Everything is okay," Malcom replied and I could literally kick him in his teeth for being such a liar.

"Really? It doesn't seem that way to me." Donovan looked over at Malcom who desperately tried to get his attitude together but failed horribly.

"Are you sure about that? Malcom why don't you tell my husband all the things you just told me." I gave him the same ugly smile that he had just given me.

I must admit, it was fun to mess with Malcom's emotions like this especially since he initially thought he had the upper hand. Even though I was still mad, it amused me to watch him back down when my husband confronted him.

"All I did was come in here to drop a few documents on your desk. I noticed that your wife had come in since the last time I had come to your office. That's all. And I was just leaving," Malcom explained then started to walk away from our little pow-wow.

"Well good. And Malcom, before you leave for the day, I will need to speak with you so don't forget to come back by here."

"Okay."

I waited until Malcom walked completely out his office completely then looked at Donovan and rolled my eyes.

"Okay. So what really just happened?" He asked as he shut the door. I took a seat in front of his desk.

"Your little assistant surely had a lot to say to me."

"What do you mean?" he asked.

"I just stopped by to take you to lunch and, when I realized you weren't here, I left you a note. He walked in just as I got ready to walk out. He was acting all funny toward me so I decided to ask him if he had a problem with me. That opened pandora's box."

"So what did he say? That he had a problem with you?"

"In so many words. He gonna call himself questioning my true motives for marrying you, saying I appeared on the scene randomly."

"What? I can't believe him."

"Donovan, I've always wanted to know, is Malcom a little sweet?" I asked. He raised his eyebrows as if he had never heard that statement.

"Absolutely not. Malcom isn't gay. Not at all. What

would make you say something like that?"

"I don't know babe. It just seems like he is a little feminine sometimes. His mannerisms and all."

Donovan chuckled when he heard me say that.

"I'm so serious. Do he have a girlfriend?"

"Listen, Denise I can assure he very much likes women. He has a little girlfriend from out of town he sees off and on. I do however not appreciate how he talked to you and the things he said are not cool. Believe me, I will handle it." I felt thankful my husband would stand up to defend me. I couldn't help but wonder if my accusations about Malcom were actually true.

Chapter 9

Terri

I pulled out my day planner while I was at work and glanced at the date on the calendar. I picked up my favorite Mont Blanc pen and added an "X" to the calendar day. I shook my head. It had been about two and a half weeks since Carlos and I had a blow up over Lily, and as a result, we weren't speaking to each other. Since we were barely speaking to each other there was no kissing, touching, rubbing and definitely no sex in that amount of time.

One day I'd came home from work like I always did and ended up getting into an argument with Lily. I came in the house and heard her talking to one of her little friends on the phone about me. She didn't know that I had come home and for a minute I didn't know where she was but I traced the sound of her voice and she was actually in my office in my leather chair with her back turned from the door. I didn't announce my presence. I stood in the doorway.

"Man, my stepmom is a trip. Got my dad living all up in the suburbs like they the Kardashians and stuff. She even got an office. That's where I'm at right now. I really didn't want to come but I did want to spend some time with my dad so I had no choice. And she tries so hard to be nice to me but she's only doing it because she has to not because she wants to. I'm surprised she even allowed me to come and stay. I know that it's only a matter of time before that's over with too. Things will change especially when she has a baby by my dad. I can kiss my daddy goodbye."

I cleared my throat loud enough for her to spin around in her chair and end her phone call. She waited to speak to me until she was off the phone.

"I heard everything you said."

"So now you're eavesdropping on me? I swear I can't have any privacy in this house." She said as she started making her way around the desk and ended up coming face to face with me.

"I'm sorry. If you're not paying the mortgage up and through here then you're not permitted any privacy. And who do you think you're talking to anyway. I'm the adult and you are the child. As far as I'm concerned, half the things you let come out of your mouth shouldn't even be said."

"I'm talking to you Terri. You act like you're my mother or something. Well, guess what you're not. And if I called my mom right now and told her how you were talking to me, she would be on the first plane from Texas."

"Lily, you can call your mom all you want to. I don't care. I'll meet her at the airport. One thing I do know is I'm not going to put up with all this disrespect. I can't wait until your father comes home."

"Wait, why do you have to put my father in this?"

"Because you insist on talking to me any kind of way and since you think that you are suddenly grown I'm going to discuss it all with your father and we will see what he thinks of it. Until then, you can go up to your room and you stay there until he gets home."

While I waited for him to come home, I just knew that my husband would have my back on this. He would be on my side after I told him how his daughter was acting. But after he came home, it was the complete opposite. Someway his daughter was able to convince him that she said none of the things I claimed she'd said and our discussion about my concerns turned into an argument. We had barely spoken to each other since. I couldn't believe Carlos had the nerve to believe that his daughter could do no wrong. I felt like she was intentionally trying to play us against each other. Regardless of what happened, I had made up in my mind that this would be the last day I would go to bed without touching my husband.

Now I'm not trying to appear like I'm a sex fiend or an addict who absolutely couldn't live without having sex but, as a married woman, I was used to getting it on a regular and going almost three weeks without it made me feel like a diabetic with low blood sugar. I needed my fix. I needed to connect with my husband. And since he was almost as stubborn as I, I made the decision that I would put an end to our strike.

After work, I stopped by my favorite lingerie store and picked up a black sheer satin bra with a matching robe and a skirt that had double thigh high splits. I paired this perfectly with my black strappy stilettos that Carlos had never seen me wear. I wanted to save them for a special occasion and what better occasion than this one right here. All of this would be saved for the ending to our night.

I picked up some light groceries and, by the time my husband walked through the door, his nostrils were bombarded with chicken parmesan and pasta. The mug that he wore on his face for the past five days was replaced with a smile. He loved chicken parmesan. It was one of his favorite dishes that I cooked. Lily and I were even getting along for the moment and I wasn't complaining about that. I was actually thankful since everything seemed to be setting things up for the perfect ending.

"I honestly thought you would be making peanut butter and jelly sandwiches the way we've been acting toward each other lately. Boy, was I surprised," he said as he cut into his first piece of chicken. When he closed his eyes to savor the bite, I knew I had him where I wanted him.

"Babe, I wasn't playing any games. When I told you I would cook your favorite, I meant exactly what I said."

"How does everything taste?" I asked Lily. I braced myself for whatever came out her mouth. Who knows what she was going to say at this point.

"It's alright. I don't really like eating stuff like

this." She picked over her plate that I. Had this been a regular day, this comment and her little attitude would've sent me over the edge but, that night, I was on a mission that didn't involve her.

"Well I'm glad you two are enjoying the food I have prepared. It's been a little while since we've been able to sit down as a family. This is nice," I said, even though I felt like giving Lily a piece of my mind. I refrained from exhibiting any of that type of negative behavior. I wasn't going to let anything or anyone come between my plans.

"May I be excused from the table daddy?" Lily rolled her eyes.

"Yes, you can be excused when you fix that attitude." In almost an instant, she changed up her expression and put a smile on her face.

"Daddy, can I pleased be excused now?" she asked again.

"Yes you can."

Carlos waited for Lily to shut her bedroom door before he opened up his mouth to speak.

"Baby, I know it hasn't been easy to deal with this situation, but I want you to know I appreciate your effort and everything you've done."

"You're welcome and you're right. It hasn't been easy but having you by my side has made everything I've gone through worthwhile." I started clearing our plates from the table.

"And I want to apologize for getting upset with you. I had no right treating you that way when it's clear my daughter has been acting a fool."

"Yeah, I'm not going to say she was acting a fool but she has definitely been trying my patience especially since she's not been completely honest with you about what she's been saying to me."

"Well I agree that she has been walking around here with an attitude but to say that she has been blatantly lying? I think that's a bit much. Don't you think?"

"So, you still believe she didn't say all those disrespectful things to me?"

"Baby, that's one thing that Lily knows that I don't tolerate and that's lying. I don't play when it comes to telling the truth. I've asked her multiple times and she tells me the same exact answer every time. I will accept many other things about my daughter but not the fact that she's a liar."

I held my hands up and shook my head. I could feel my attitude returning that I was trying so hard to get rid of so we could make amends.

"Before we start to get into it again, I realize that we don't have to see eye to eye on this issue. I'm going to apologize again for my part in handling things." I offered.

"Apology accepted. And I want to apologize for how I've been acting toward you these past few days. It was immature of me to stay this upset at you for so long. I am sorry." Carlos replied.

"Baby, I forgive you," I said as he brought the cups from the table to the sink where I stood. Carlos leaned in and kissed me. It felt good to even have our lips touching again. I'm not going to lie. My frustration was growing toward Lily and Carlos. I felt like they were a part of some sick team to gang up against me. He was blind to the fact that his daughter was clearly playing him and his daughter was playing him like a fiddle. In this moment, I could choose to continue to be mad at my husband and waste this night that I had planned or I could continue on with my original plans and since I was ready to move forward I chose the latter.

"That's why I wanted to cook you dinner as a way to say I'm sorry and I also have something planned for us a little later." I kissed my husband back and told him I would give him the signal when I was ready for the next part of our evening. He had a few things to finish up in his office so I told him that would be perfect. That would give Lily time to go to sleep. I went upstairs ran myself a nice, hot bubble bath and took my time letting the steaminess of the water take me to a place of relaxation. I put on some soft jazz, turned my Jacuzzi jets on, and allowed myself to sink down in the tub until my neck rested just above the level of the water.

Once I stepped out of my bath, I dried myself off with a towel, put on my ensemble, and then began to set the ambiance. I pulled up one of my smooth jazz mixes on my iPod and let that play softly in the background. I lit the various candles I had previously placed all over the room. I dimmed the lights and just as I was getting ready to text Carlos, he strolled through our bedroom door. His eyes were immediately drawn to my new ensemble. I twirled around in a circle modeling my new piece for him.

"And why were we mad at each other again? Carlos walked up to me and held me in his arms.

"I'm having the hardest time remembering." I leaned myself upward so I could kiss him. Being in my husband's arms had to be the best feeling in the world. His strong, chiseled arms lifted my body up to the point where I could wrap my legs around him. He brought me over to our king size bed and laid me down. He began kissing me from head to toe. His hands worked on removing my lingerie piece by piece until nothing remained.

My body craved him. I missed his touch. I missed his mouth tasting my innermost treasure. I felt myself entering into another zone but we were interrupted by Lily screaming at the top of her lungs. Hearing her scream sent a chill up and down my spine. Carlos left our bedroom and took off running down the hallway toward her. After I threw some clothes on, I followed suit. When I reached her room, I found Carlos sitting on the side of the bed consoling Lily who appeared to be crying. She was all engrossed in her tears and they were magnified once I stepped in the room. I pay attention to everything.

"What's going on?" I asked as I pulled my robe tighter.

"Baby, she's alright. She said she had a nightmare or something."

"Yeah, Ms. Terri. I had the craziest dream but I'm fine now that daddy came and checked on me." Her frown of sadness seemed to turn into pure contentment right before my eyes. Upon looking at her, it became evident that this little girl didn't have a doggone nightmare. I could clearly decipher what happened and this little girl had just put on the performance of a lifetime and succeeded because she had definitely killed my entire vibe. I wasn't in the mood to do anything especially not with my husband.

"Thank you for checking on me, Ms. Terri. I really appreciate it." Lily gave me her signature fake smile and it took everything within me not to react.

"No problem. Carlos, I'm going to bed." I walked out of the room, then marched back down the hall, climbed in bed and stared at the clock on my nightstand. I couldn't believe my plans were derailed just that fast all because of a lie. That girl knows good and darn well she didn't have a nightmare. She was in her room crying crocodile tears like she was in the middle of an audition for a day time soap opera. Twenty minutes later my husband came back into our bedroom, thinking he would pick up where we left off but I pretended to be sleep. Carlos could blame my sudden sleepiness on his daughter's stellar performance.

Chapter 10

Denise

I was hanging out in the kitchen with our chef, as he made spaghetti, when Donovan walked through the door. He was visibly upset and his frustration he wore on his face.

"Hey baby, what's wrong?" I asked him as he began to flip through mail.

"Nothing. I really don't want to talk about it." Donovan continued opening mail.

"Come on, honey. You know you can always talk to me. What's going on with you?" I asked again.

Donovan took a deep breath and then exhaled.

"I decided to let go of Malcom today."

"What happened?"

"I confronted him about what went down between you two at the church."

"Well, I assumed you two would have a conversation. I never thought that would be the end result of everything."

"I didn't either, but the bottom line is, I can't have him around if he's going to disrespect you like that. Him disrespecting you is in turn being disrespectful to me."

"Why do you feel he's like that?" I asked.

"You know at this point I don't know and I don't care. With him being gone, it's going to be difficult. And even though not having him around is going to be a challenge, I would rather it be a struggle than to have to deal with the blatant disrespect."

"Hopefully, you will find a replacement soon. On another note our dinner is ready. Are you ready to eat?" I went over to start setting the table.

"Babe, to be honest, I'm not hungry at all. I'm gonna turn in early. Sorry." He went upstairs to our master bedroom. I couldn't say that I was glad Malcom lost his job. But I'm not going to lie, I was kind of relieved that Malcom and his jacked up attitude wouldn't be around nearly as much. I was even more relieved that my husband had my back and stood up for me. I know it was hard for him to let go the best assistant he'd ever had but I would definitely find a way to make it up to him. After I finished working my magic on him, he would forget that Malcom ever existed.

Once I was finished with eating dinner and putting Kaylah to bed, I joined my husband. I slipped in and wrapped my arms around him in an attempt to cuddle but Donovan tensed up his body and turned in the opposite direction away from me. I moved closer to him and rolled my body toward him then tried to snuggle up close to him again but he jerked away from me. Everything within me wanted to be offended, to think he was being cold towards me, but I decided to not take it so personal. Besides, he was in such a deep sleep that he probably wasn't aware of his own actions. I turned over to my side of the bed and closed my eyes.

The next morning, I could feel Donovan's eyes staring at me but I continued to sleep. I was too tired to even figure out why he had already woken up.

"Denise, let's make a baby." Donovan's statement caused my eyes to pop open. He totally caught me by surprise! I wasn't even aware it was morning. I must've been really tired because the last thing I remembered was getting into bed and I tried my hardest to cuddle with him and show him some affection but he was so upset from the night before and firing Malcom that he wasn't having it at all. So for him to wake up and immediately ask for a baby kind of caught me off guard.

"Good morning, to you too." I studied his countenance to see if he was being serious and he didn't even flinch.

"I'm serious, babe. I am so thankful to have Kaylah in my life and, while I will raise her as if she's mine, it still has created a desire in me to have one of my own as well."

"I understand what you're saying but don't you think it's a little soon to be trying to have kids, don't you think?" I asked him and couldn't be more confused my own self. This was the same man who was so pissed off the night before that he didn't even want to eat or cuddle. Now, he's super focused on growing our family. This man flipped his mood faster than you could flip a television channel.

"No I don't think it's too soon. In my eyes it will never be the right time to start a family so let's start now."

"I'm trying to figure out where is all this talk of having kids is coming from. You never mentioned having children when we were just dating."

"I know I haven't really mentioned it much but being in love with you and being married to you has heightened my desire to have a child."

We had never talked about having children and actually I didn't think we ever would. With Donovan having such a hectic travel schedule and my own personal disdain for not ever wanting to be pregnant ever again, I just figured that we would never cross that bridge.

"Okay well I'm not opposed to starting a family." I lied.

"I just need a little time to think about it. That's all."

"How can I argue with that? I will give you all the time you need. It's time for me to get up and get moving. I will be taping a few episodes for the Light Network today so we will have to catch a late dinner. Hopefully, afterwards, we can get a head start on trying to have a baby." He winked at me and went in the bathroom. I was glad he had chosen to get ready for the day. That way, I wouldn't have to fabricate or lie anymore. There was no way in hell I would have any more kids and that little conversation was confirmation enough that I needed to make an appointment with a gynecologist so that I could get back on birth control as soon as possible.

Kaylah decided, after I got her dressed, that she wanted to have a tea party so that's exactly what we did. We made a cute spread on the living room floor and set up a nice tea party for us and her stuffed animals too. We were having a good old time until we were interrupted by the door bell ringing.

"Stay here sweetie. I'll be right back," I said as I hurried to the door.

"Are you Mrs. Rodgers?" The mailman asked me.

"Yes, I am." I answered.

"I have a certified letter for you. Can you please sign here?" He handed me an electronic device to sign. Once I did, he handed me the letter and said, "Have a nice day ma'am."

I closed the door and started to examine the envelope. The letter was addressed to me but it didn't have any return address. I shrugged it off and opened it up anyway. Inside was a crumpled letter that the unknown sender had desperately tried to straighten. I found it strange that the letter had been previously addressed to someone else but their name was ripped out. I sat down in the living room and started to read it.

I know you weren't expecting a letter from me but I figured I would surprise you. I had the most amazing time with you and I must say that you totally caught me by surprise. I have been attracted to you for some time but struggled with actually revealing it to you. I was apprehensive due to the fact of not knowing if you felt the same way I did. And I never thought that you did but this past weekend confirmed what I was feeling was mutual between us. I've always enjoyed being in your presence but even more now that we've actually spent time together. You went above and beyond to make sure our time together was unforgettable. I honestly don't know what you and I are but I am intrigued by what's developing between us. I just need some time to figure our situation out. One thing I can promise is that I will never hurt you. My only request is that you keep this between us.

Donovan

We were only a month into our marriage, and I was receiving letters he had supposedly written to someone. I know he was in the spotlight and things like this were bound to happen but I don't know if I was actually ready to deal with the foolishness that came along with me being married to such a prominent person. I would definitely be bringing this letter to his attention the minute he came home. This letter would serve as our current conversation piece. And I wasn't stupid, I wouldn't assume anything. I was prepared to let him explain it all, especially since his signature was clearly signed at the end. If I was anxious about anything, I was anxious about that. I couldn't wait to see what he was going to say to the piece of mail that came for him.

Chapter 11

Randy

"Thanks for agreeing to meet me. I know you may find this a little strange but I thought we should get to know each other since your daughter is living with me," Donovan explained as he sat across from me at the Cheesecake Factory. I didn't consider our lunch meeting strange however I did raise my eyebrow at the email he mysteriously sent me, telling me he purchased an earlier first class flight so he and I could meet up. Up until this point, I had never even had a conversation with the man and here he's taken it upon himself to email me. I considered that to be a bit backwards since they were already married but I respected him for wanting to get to know me anyway. And I was actually excited to be able to see my daughter and spend some more time with her. It had been about five weeks since I had flown down to drop her off and I missed not being able to see her every day.

"Oh, I don't find it strange. Actually, I'm glad that we got a chance to get together. I'm a very hands-on type of guy. I like to know who's in my daughter's life," I replied.

"I totally understand. If I had a daughter I would be the same way. By the way, it has been such a joy having Kaylah in my life. She's such a beautiful little girl."

"Thank you. That's my baby girl right there. I wished she didn't have to live so far away but I'm not in charge with the decisions Denise makes so I just have to deal with it."

I would be lying if I said having my daughter live out of state was easy because it's not. Besides divorcing Denise, being apart from Kaylah has been one of the hardest things I've had to do. It's hard to see the person you love live so far away and, although Denise hurt me by moving my child so far away, I had been dealing with the best way I knew how. With Kaylah not actually being my biological child you would think that I would take Denise moving across states as an opportunity to be completely free from her and all of the drama that surrounds her but I wasn't that type of man. As far as I was concerned, Kaylah was my daughter with no other additional questions needing to be asked. My bond with my daughter was just as strong as if she were actually my daughter for real.

"So you have a problem with Denise living here in Florida?" he asked me.

"It's not that I have a problem. It's just her moving her so far away has made it difficult for me to be an active part of my child's life but with Denise making this move it's not surprising at all."

"Well if you were so concerned about being a part of Kaylah's life then why did you even divorce Denise in the first place? You know she's told me everything that happened between you two." Donovan spoke with a straight attitude laced in his voice.

I should've known that this first class flight and secret lunch had an ulterior motive other than serving the sole purpose as a way of getting to know each other. He wanted to play twenty-one questions with me.

"Well, if your wife has told you everything, you should know why I divorced her." I picked up my glass and took a drink of water while I waited for his rebuttal. I also wondered if she had been honest about everything. I wondered if she had been honest about the infidelity, the paternity of our daughter, and the multiple affairs.

"Enlighten me." Donovan crossed his arms over the table and leaned in like he was getting ready to participate in story time.

"My decision to divorce Denise wasn't an easy one believe me. I would've given anything to keep my family together but, after she betrayed my trust, we had to go our separate ways. It was the best thing to do."

"She betrayed your trust?"

"She cheated on me a few times. Listen, I don't know what she's told you and frankly I don't care. I'm not even trying to involve myself in your personal business. I'm just trying to remain in contact with my daughter. That's all."

"Don't worry, Randy. My wife told me everything. There are no secrets between us. I don't know what your relationship was like with her but mine couldn't be better."

"From the look on your face I can't tell."

What I said clearly bothered him. I don't care if he wanted to front like things were okay. I knew deep down inside they weren't and what he was showing me was just on the surface. The reason why he'd become so defensive revealed the actual truth more than anything else. Denise had never told him. Knowing her, she probably made up all kinds of lies about me and what I had supposedly done to her. Honestly, I could care less about what Denise had to say about me. It wasn't like I wanted to be back in her life anyway.

"My facial expression isn't giving off anything other than the fact that it's obvious that you're jealous that your wife is with me." He laughed and I laughed too simply because I couldn't believe that he actually had the guts to say this to me. I could see why they felt they were a match made in heaven. He was just as delusional.

"So you think I'm jealous of you? How do you figure that?"

"You're jealous because you actually let Denise get away and now she's with someone who treats her better than you ever did."

"Excuse me? You're implying that I didn't treat Denise good? Now Denise can tell you whatever your listening ears want to hear but I will not let you sit here and attack my character and you don't even know me. For the record, when Denise was my wife, I treated her very well. I'm the one who chose to end our marriage and I did so for a specific reason. Before you go of accusing me of things, you need to have all of your facts straight instead of her fabricated version of her reality." I replied trying to pull myself together because the way I was feeling I could've reached over the table and had my fist meet his face. Donovan stared in my eyes and then leaned back in his seat.

"I must say, I enjoy verbal sparring almost as much as I enjoy preaching." He smiled obviously pleased with seeing me upset.

"Donovan, with all due respect, I didn't come here to hurl insults back and forth with you. If that's what this lunch was about then I'm out of here." I attempted to get up from the table but he stopped me.

"Come on, Randy. Sit back down. Of course, I didn't invite you out for all this. I really did want to meet you and just get my own personal feeling for you. I didn't mean for it to go this way. I extend my sincerest apology." He held out his hand and stretched it across the table.

I shook his hand and sat back down.

"You're forgiven." I answered.

As we ate lunch, we made small talk. We talked about ministry, travelling, and discussing different places we've visited. I excused myself from the table momentarily to use the restroom. I needed a break from the tension that built up during lunch. As I made my way back toward our table, I could see Donovan engaged in a deep conversation on his cell phone. Immediately, I assumed he was talking to Denise. It took me a few minutes to navigate the aisle leading back to our table. By the time I made it within ear shot, I heard Donovan proclaim, "Don't worry. We'll spend some time together so stop calling me." He ended his call, when he saw me.

"Denise calling you already?" I tried to joke with him.

"That wasn't Denise," he replied.

"Oh," I said as the waitress brought us our bill. Donovan slid the check over to him and pulled out his credit card to cover our bill.

"That was actually my nephew. Little man always trying to spend time with his uncle and doesn't understand that I have to work."

"Sounded like you were arguing."

Donovan laughed. "That's just how we talk to each other."

I shook my head as if I agreed but it didn't take a genius to know that the person on the other end wasn't his nephew.

"Really? Okay, if you say so."

"You're trying to imply that I'm lying. Randy, I thought we would take this time to get to know each other, since we have been forced to be in each other's lives to some capacity. I never imagined that you would come here and accuse me of something that I am not even capable of."

"I'm not accusing you of anything. You're taking offense to an assumption."

"I'm not assuming anything. Your tone suggests that you don't believe I was talking with my nephew." He said with his jaws clenched and nostrils flaring.

"Why are you so upset? You told me who you were talking to and that's the end of it. I guess I'll take that as my cue to get back to the hotel and rest up. Donovan, it's all good. Thanks for lunch." I got up from the table and shook his hand even though he clearly didn't want to return the gesture. Looking at Donovan's countenance and overall attitude confirmed that I in fact had caught him in a lie.

Chapter 12

Denise

"Does this letter look familiar to you?" I handed him the letter I'd previously received in the mail across the table as we sat eating breakfast. Donovan opened the crumpled piece of paper and began scanning it with his eyes.

"No where did you get this letter from? It doesn't look familiar to me." He handed the letter back to me.

"I find it funny that you can sit here and say that you don't remember this letter when it's clearly your handwriting and you even signed it at the bottom. Do you think I'm stupid or something?" I asked. Donovan turned to Kaylah, "Princess, can you go to your room. Papa will be up there in a second to watch your favorite show before I leave, okay?"

"Okay papa." Kaylah smiled and then ran up the steps.

"Now back to what you were saying. You think I wrote that letter?" He asked. His nonchalant attitude only angered me more.

"Of course I think you wrote it. Your name is right there and this is clearly your handwriting. You can't slide out of this one."

"There's nothing to slide out of as far as I'm concerned, because I didn't write the letter. How did you even get this letter anyway?"

"It was sent to the house certified mail. It's obvious that someone wanted me to have this letter you sent them. Just tell the truth, Donovan."

"I am telling the truth. If you think I'm such a liar then why did you marry me? I'm not about to sit here and go back and forth with you. Now if you'll excuse me I'm going to watch a little TV with Kaylah before I have to get to church."

"Whatever." I rolled my eyes.

"Oh, and I'll see you later for lunch."

I could sit and try to call myself being upset because of Donovan's nonchalant response but all that would do was make me look even more crazier than I already did. Maybe I was tripping or insecure because I had been unfaithful in my past. Whatever it was I felt silly even bringing it to his attention in the first place. Randy ended up texting me right after Donovan left and said that he was rested up from flying into town yesterday. So we agreed to meet out for lunch. I ended up getting Kaylah ready to see her daddy. And her being the inquisitive little three year old she is had decided just what she wanted to put on to see her daddy.

"Mommy, I want to wear my yellow dress." She insisted as I stood in front of her walk-in closet staring at her outfits.

"Okay sweetie. You're going to look so pretty in your yellow for daddy."

I made sure I added yellow ribbons to her ponytails and then I put on one of her favorite movies on her TV for her to watch while I got myself ready. It wasn't until I went into my bathroom that I started feeling like I was coming down with something. My stomach felt queasy and if I had a full stomach I probably would've vomited its contents all over the marble floors in my bathroom. If I didn't have anything on my agenda for the day I would definitely be staying inside but that wasn't an option for me. I shrugged off the nauseous feeling due to the fact that it was probably my nerves trying to get the best of me.

"How was your flight? I asked Randy. We sat across from each other at Brio. We met Randy out for lunch the day after he flew in town. I was actually glad to see him. It allowed me to focus on something else other than Donovan.

"My flight wasn't that bad. The drive to my hotel was a trip."

"The driver was new. Almost killed me on the way to the hotel. He was swerving all over the highway, claiming he just moved here and doesn't know his way around the city. I never prayed so hard in my life." Randy laughed and I smiled.

One year ago I couldn't even stand to talk to him let alone be in the same room. Time definitely has a way of changing things. He was still handsome as ever and dressed to impress as always. I noticed there was a difference in his style and, although I hated to admit it, he looked real good. Of course I would never tell Randy to his face but I liked the change. His jeans were a little more relaxed but they fit his body perfectly. He wore a crispy white V-cut T-shirt that revealed that he had been hitting the gym lately. He even carried himself with more confidence. He had a new found swag that stood out to me and made him look a little sexy to me.

This man is your ex-husband not a potential prospect. Keep it together girl.

I had to admit. I still loved him, probably even more than I loved Donovan. I had to remind my own doggone self I couldn't look at Randy in that light anymore. But him looking all scrumptious, sitting across from me, made it almost darn near impossible.

"So I must say I'm still a bit shocked you are a married woman... again. Congratulations." Randy said as he examined my wedding ring. He offered a slight smile and nodded his head as some sort of approval. I don't know why he was fronting. My ring was the absolute truth.

"Thank you, Randy. When a situation is right, it doesn't take too long to make things happen."

"Believe me I don't have anything to say other than I'm happy for you two. Speaking of, where's Donovan? I thought he was supposed to meet us out here."

I glanced down at my watch and figured he would still be caught up with his work.

"You know what? I don't know. He was supposed to meet us here but maybe he is still at the church." I lied. I hoped Donovan didn't remember to meet us here at the restaurant or got too caught up in his work to come. I didn't even want to see his face right now. Just when I thought he wouldn't show up, he appeared and Kaylah rushed out of her seat to greet him. So much for my hopes and dreams.

"Hi papa!" Kaylah said as she wrapped her arms around his legs and gave him a hug.

"Hey princess, are you going sit by me?" he asked. She shook her head no.

"No, I'm gonna sit with my daddy." She walked back over to Randy and he pulled out the chair next to him. Donovan had a weird look on his face.

"So glad you're here, honey. Donovan, this is Randy. Randy, this is my husband Donovan." It sounded weird to introduce my new husband to my ex-husband.

"I'm sorry I'm late but I got caught up finalizing some contracts for future speaking engagements," Donovan explained and I cut my eyes at him on the sly. I wondered if he was actually telling the truth or was lying about this too.

"I totally understand. You must be super busy with speaking all over the country and having a television show. How do you find time for family?" Randy asked.

"I make time. It's all about having balance. Right before I met Denise, my life was very hectic. But I remember praying and asking the Lord to show me how to make room for a wife and a family. And, he did." Randy shook his head with satisfaction.

"Oh I almost forgot, I had a present for you and Kaylah." He reached in his pocket and pulled out two small boxes. He handed me a slender rectangular box and my daughter a smaller one. The light teal blue boxes were a dead giveaway that the gifts were from Tiffany's. I smiled when I opened it and saw the diamond bracelet I had been eyeing. I looked over at Kaylah who finally opened hers. She received a pair of diamond earrings. For the way I had been treating him lately, a gift was a nice peace offering. And let's be clear, just because I accepted his gift doesn't mean that he was back in my good graces.

"Mommy look at my earrings! Thank you Papa!" Kaylah smiled.

"You're welcome Princess."

"It's beautiful. Thank you." I replied as he took the bracelet off and fastened it around my wrist. Randy then gave me the weirdest look but turned his attention toward our daughter and helped her to put her earrings in. Talk about an awkward moment. I acted as though Randy wasn't giving me strange looks. As far as I was concerned, he couldn't be mad at the fact God decided to bless me. It wasn't my fault that God still saw fit to bless me even though my previous actions caused an end to my first marriage. Yes, things weren't perfect in my current marriage but, regardless, it was my situation and Randy wasn't entitled to know my personal business.

"So how long are you here for?" Donovan asked

as he put his arm around the back of my chair and pulled me close. Luckily, I wanted to save face in front of Randy otherwise I would've moved my chair away from him.

"I'll be here for the next three days."

"Ok well Denise and I would love to have you over for dinner at our home before you go."

After lunch Randy decided to take Kaylah with him for the rest of the day. I was on my way home when my gynecologist office called me to let me know they had a cancellation and could fit me in if I could get there. I turned my car around and made it there within fifteen minutes. With Donovan getting the baby itch, I made it my top priority to protect myself. We had been using condoms before we got married but ever since we he wanted to start having a baby, he refused to wear them. I had been timing everything perfectly around my ovulation period but I would only be able to do that for so long. Now, it was time to get some birth control.

"Mrs. Rodgers, the doctor will see you now." The secretary opened the door and led me to a room. Before I met with the doctor, the medical assistant drew my blood for lab work and I provided my urine sample. She then led me to an examination room and told me the doctor would be in to see me shortly.

As I waited for her, I browsed through my phone, checked a few of my emails and I even received a picture from Kaylah that her father sent me. I was surprised she still hadn't come in to see me. I wondered what took her so long. Just when I planned to go back out to the front desk, the doctor entered wearing a smile.

"Mrs. Rodgers, congratulations."

"Congratulations for what?" I curiously asked. I really hope she was going to tell me my birth control prescription was cheap.

"I know you initially came here to get back on your birth control but you actually won't be needing that for at least the next nine months. You're pregnant."

"I'm pregnant? There's no way I can be pregnant. I haven't been sick or gained any weight. How is this possible?"

Now I knew how this happened but I was just puzzled at the fact that I was pregnant and didn't even know it. Even though I had previously been in denial when I was pregnant with Kaylah I still knew that something was going on with my body. If I was pregnant I would've known. I felt no symptoms.

"Well , your urine and blood tests were both positive so you're definitely pregnant. Now I would have to actually schedule you for a sonogram to confirm how far along you are but, judging from when you had your last period, I would say you're probably around six weeks," The doctor explained. "I bet your husband is going to be thrilled."

"Ecstatic." I wasn't exactly thrilled or excited to be with child once again. I hadn't actually planned on having any more children so hearing this news made me the opposite of excited. I was totally blindsided to say the least. I definitely couldn't tell Donovan this right now. I have to keep this from him until I figure out what I planned to do. I traced back on the calendar in my phone and realized that

I had in fact gotten pregnant during our time in Vegas. *So much for being careful*, I thought.

Even though I made a pit stop to the doctor's office, I still ended up arriving at home before Donovan. We hadn't spent any time alone since that mysterious letter arrived. I was still livid that he claimed he didn't write the letter in spite of his signature. I went down to our gym to get a good sweat in and release some of the frustration I had inside of me. I was in the middle of my routine on the elliptical when Donovan came walking through the door. He made sure he made eye contact with me and then started to laugh.

"What?" I asked and he continued to laugh like someone had told him the funniest joke ever.

"So that's the dude you married huh?"

"Yeah, what's wrong with that?"

"Nothing, I can just see why two didn't last. That's all."

"Whatever, that's easy for you to say. You barely even know him."

"I don't have to be the man's best friend to know that he's absolutely not on your level. You honestly should be glad that you're not married to that guy anymore. I don't want to toot my own horn, but I was surely your upgrade." Donovan stated. I rolled my eyes and shook my head. His cockiness made me sick at times.

"I swear you're ridiculous." I continued on with my workout like he wasn't there.

"So you're still upset about that letter aren't you?"

"Yeah, why wouldn't I be? I mean I still don't understand how a letter can contain your handwriting and your very own signature and you know nothing about it. I'm still having a hard time understanding that. I swear I don't even know who you are sometimes." I confessed.

"It's funny to hear you say, you don't know who I am. I feel the same way after talking to your husband."

"What are you talking about?" I asked totally confused at his comment.

"Your husband and I had an interesting conversation about you and he seemed to have a very different version of the story you told me about how you two broke up. Now I know the real reason why you stay accusing me of cheating on you. You did the same thing to him."

"I can't believe you two had a conversation about me."

"Initially, we weren't trying to but God has an amazing way of always revealing the truth doesn't he?"

"So you believe what Randy told you about me?"

"I'm not saying I totally believe him but he definitely opened my eyes to some things. I understand you're mad about this letter and what you think I'm supposedly doing out here but you're not exactly an angel either. If you say you trust me, then you have to trust me. I mean I trust you even when I have reasons not to. I'm telling you, it wasn't me. Do you know how many lunatics exist in this world? I always receive crazy things that are mailed to me. And if they are not mailed here then they are mailed to the church.

This one letter isn't the first and isn't the last. Here take a look at this." Donovan waited for me to jump off the elliptical machine then handed me a stack of letters and cards. There were correspondence from all over the world, people saying some crazy stuff. Some letters even stated that he had actual relationships with these crazy women.

"You see what I'm talking about? Now, if you believed every single letter that I received you wouldn't be able to keep up with it all. I understand receiving stuff like this makes you upset but this kind of stuff comes along with the territory. Since you're my wife that makes you just as much as a target as me. You cannot flip out every time someone decides to send a letter. What are you going to do when these same lunatics discover your phone number and start calling you up? You gonna run to divorce me? You have to put things in the proper perspective and quit being so quick to assume. Sometimes our assumptions will have us caught up into some situations."

"I guess, Donovan. This is just a lot to handle." Oddly enough, I started to cry. *What the hell was I crying for? Then I remembered that heightened emotions was a part of pregnancy.*

"Baby, I know that being married to me has been quite an adjustment but I promise you I made you my wife because I am in love with you. I wouldn't do you like that. I'm trying to be married until we're old and gray and can't even remember each other's names. You don't have to worry about me out here dipping and diving. I am in love with you, Mrs. Rodgers." Donovan leaned down and gave me one of the most passionate kisses ever.

"I love you too, Mr. Rodgers," I replied through a smile and I felt reassured as I looked in his eyes. I always felt like I could really read a person by looking them square in the eyes. His eyes showed me that he was sincere. It felt like he was being for real. Our love was for real.

Donovan pulled me in his arms and everything felt so right.

"Now, since we've made up let's go and make me a son." He winked. That's when he reminded me of the news I had just received. I was already six weeks pregnant with our first child together and while I should be celebrating the fact that our family was expanding, I was far from the celebratory mood. I pressed my lips together and offered a stiff smile. No matter how many times I tried to get excited about being pregnant, I couldn't.

At this point I wasn't even sure that I wanted to keep it. Since my pregnancy was still early on there were a lot of things working out in my favor. I wasn't showing any signs of being with child. I hadn't gained any weight. I wasn't experiencing morning sickness or weird hunger cravings. I could honestly have an abortion and Donovan would never even suspect anything. Either way, I decided to keep this information from my husband until I figured out whether I was going to keep our child or get rid of it.

Chapter 13

Terri

I came home from a long day at the office and found Lily sitting on the couch in the living room flipping through a magazine. I arrived home before Carlos did. The garage smelled a little like smoke. I noticed it the minute I pulled in but I attributed it to the summer time and everyone in our neighborhood had been outside on their patios grilling. I opened the door to the house and was hit with the familiar smell of smoke again.

"Hello Lily, how was your day?" I asked even though she was the last person I wanted to talk to. She paused for a moment as if she wasn't going to answer me. Then she closed her magazine and set it down in front of her on the coffee table. Lily's behavior led me to believe she acted disrespectful on purpose, as though her life's mission was to make my life absolutely miserable.

"It was cool, I've just been sitting here." She replied with a smirk on her face. The way she smiled at me didn't sit right with me so I decided to cut straight to the punch with her.

"Why does it smell like smoke in here?"

Lily shrugged her shoulders.

"I dunno. I don't smell any smoke." She answered.

"Come on Lily. That's the first thing I smelled when I walked through the door. So where is it coming from?" I asked *again*.

"I don't know what you're talking about, I've been here in the living room all day."

Not accepting her answer, I walked the entire first floor of the house in search of the smoky stench. The entire time I pursued the smell, Lily stood there with her hand on her skinny hip as if she had an attitude. I looked in every corner, closet and inch of the downstairs and didn't find anything. The last place I decided to check was my garage. I remembered that being the first place I smelled it. I discovered a black trash bag in the corner away from the door. I didn't remember it being there before I left for work. I walked over to the bag and looked inside. I almost fainted when I saw my favorite pair of nude *Christian Louboutin* pumps burned up inside. I grabbed the bag and stormed back inside the house.

"Do you mind telling me what happened to my shoes?" I asked as I picked them up out of the bag and dropped them on the kitchen floor.

"Oh those shoes. They got burnt when I made a

grilled cheese sandwich earlier." I definitely wasn't buying that stupid excuse.

"Lily, do you think I was born yesterday? There is no way my shoes got burned like that At least, if you are going to lie, please make up a better one than that."

"So now you're calling me a liar? I didn't lie. That's what really happened to your stupid shoes." Lily sucked her teeth and smacked her lips.

"You know what!" I said and then stopped myself before I lost it all and snatched her up. I took my shoes, threw them back in the bag and then walked outside and sat on the front porch. I waited until Carlos got home from work. When he pulled in the driveway and saw me sitting there, he parked his car outside the garage and came up the sidewalk to meet me.

"What are you doing out here?" he asked.

"I'm out here so I won't go to jail for putting my hands on that little girl in there."

"Babe, what's going on?"

"When I came home from work, I found Lily flipping through a magazine. But as we were talking, I kept smelling smoke. Once I traced my steps, I found this." I handed him the black trash bag. He opened it and seemed at a loss for words.

"What happened? How did they get burnt?" he asked.

"Lily burnt them, Carlos. She tried to feed me some bogus story making herself a grilled cheese sandwich or something. I'm no Betty Crocker, even Ray Charles could see right through that lie."

"Babe, you honestly think she would burn your shoes intentionally?"

For a second, all I could do was just look at him. I couldn't believe he actually questioned whether his daughter damaged my favorite shoes or not.

"What other reason would she have? I remember those particular pair of shoes being upstairs in our closet so she had to intentionally go upstairs and grab them and intentionally set them on fire. So yes, I believe Lily intentionally ruined my shoes," I stated.

"Ok, let's go in and talk to her right now." I followed behind him as he walked in the house and found his daughter sitting in the same exact spot. This time, she was on her phone.

"Mom, I'm going to call you back. Dad just walked in the house." She ended her phone call.

"Terri came home and found this. Would you mind filling me in on how these shoes got this way?" He dropped the bag on the floor at her feet and then put his hands in both of his pockets.

"Dad, they got messed up when I was making a grilled cheese sandwich earlier. I left a dish towel to close to the fire on the stove and it caught on fire. When I tried to put it out, I ended up using her shoes to stomp it out. I didn't want the fire to spread."

"So you're saying that you didn't mess up your stepmother's shoes on purpose"

"No. I would never do that. I know those are some

expensive shoes. I would never do that, daddy." Lily looked over at my husband who obviously believed this little stupid story. I couldn't believe he didn't see straight through her. Maybe it was the lawyer in me. Carlos then turned to me.

"Baby, see I knew this was some misunderstanding." He tried to reason with me and I wasn't having it at all. And if I couldn't get any more pissed at the situation, Lily came up to me.

"Ms. Terri," She said, "I'm very sorry I messed up your shoes today. I know you're upset and I didn't mean to make you upset. Please accept my apology." Lily gave me the fakest smile and apology I had ever seen. It took everything within me not to snatch her up right then and there.

"I accept your apology," I replied and then went to the kitchen and grabbed my Michael Kors purse. Carlos ended up following right behind me.

"Hey babe, where you going?" he asked.

"I'm going for a drive. I'll be back." I walked through the kitchen to the garage, got in my car and left. Usually, when pissed about something, I could just drive over Denise's house. But, with her out of state, that wasn't an option for me anymore. So rather than stay in the house and snap, I figured I would take a nice long drive around Millcreek Park.

I couldn't believe Lily was acting the way she did. At this point, it wasn't even about my expensive pair of shoes. I had been going out of my way and above and beyond to make sure she felt comfortable in my home and hoped we could at least start building a relationship together . But, it seemed like every time I tried and we took a step forward something happened that made us take ten steps back. I knew her mother despised the ground I walked on. I at least thought that once Lily came with us for the summer, she would warm up to the idea that I would be in her life. Now I could see that was definitely not going to happen. I pulled out my cell phone and called my best friend.

"Girl, I'm so glad you answered. Please tell me why I had to leave my house and go on a drive?'

"Terri what's going on?"

I explained to Denise what was going on and she couldn't believe what her ears were hearing.

"Oooooh. That's not good. I would've went off too. I know how you are when it comes to your shoes. How did she burn them up?"

"I don't know what she exactly did to burn them up but she tried to give me some bogus lie, especially when my stove is electric. You know I've heard criminals who lie better than her." I went on to tell her Carlos' response.

"I know you were hot Terri."

"Yes, hot isn't even the word. The fact that he actually believed her took my anger to another level. But I didn't want this whole conversation to be about me. How are things with you and Donovan?" I asked.

"Girl, I don't even know what to say right now. Donovan has really been acting very mysterious lately. I've been discovering some things that makes me question a few things about him. And on top of all that, I am pregnant again. Can you believe that?"

My best friend had just given me a complete ear full. Here I was, calling to complain about some shoes and she was going through far worse things than I.

"Wow. You're pregnant? I already know you aren't happy about that. You swore up and down that Kaylah was your one and only."

"Oh don't worry she is. That won't change."

"What are you talking about? How does Donovan feel about you being pregnant?"

"He doesn't know just yet. As far as I'm concerned I am keeping this one to myself. I don't even think I'm having this baby. I'm really contemplating getting an abortion."

"Denise, are you serious? Why would you abort a child that's perfectly fine? There's no reason why you would have to do that? You're married and this is a totally different situation than before. I could understand why you were apprehensive about having a baby the first time but times have changed."

"I understand but that still doesn't change my mind about having this baby. I know that you prefer me not to get rid of it but I'm still not convinced on continuing this pregnancy."

"Please think about what you just said long and hard before you decide to do something like that. You know how lies and deception destroyed your first marriage I would hate to see the same thing happen all over again.

You know I'm only saying it because I love you."

"Yes, I know you do and I love you too. I am really going to think about this like you said but with all this drama that is currently going on can you blame me? I just want to hold on to this for a little while longer until I figure out what I'm going to do."

Chapter 14

Denise

I was awakened by Donovan holding a tray full of breakfast food and a smile. I yawned and asked, "What's all this for?"

"Good morning baby. I wanted to bring breakfast in bed to you. You like?" He asked.

"Of course. The food smells amazing. Did you cook this?"

"No but you must applaud my effort though." He laughed.

"Your effort is duly noted. You know I can get really used to you catering to me. So I'm really about to enjoy this moment." I replied and then sat up and smoothed the covers so he could set the tray across my lap.

"Well I'm glad you're enjoying this because today is a special day."

"It is?"

"Yes, today it's all about you."

"Donovan, what do you have planned?"

"Don't worry about it, my love. I just need you to eat breakfast so I can get you moving along today."

"Oh okay. I'm good at following directions." I started to eat my breakfast. I began to smile when I thought of the possibilities of what he planned for me. I could tell he had something up his sleeve and I liked it. After I ate my food, Donovan told me to get dressed. Downstairs, he revealed the next part of the surprise.

"Okay, baby. The car service is outside to take you to the spa for a full day of pampering. When you're done there, you will go to the salon and get your hair done. So enjoy." He kissed me on my lips and opened the door. A limo waited for me.

"You're sneaky and I love it." I replied before walking out. With all the arguing we had done lately, being pampered for the day felt nice for a change. I was able to stop thinking about all that had been recently going on.

The driver took me to this lovely all inclusive spa and the staff gave me the works a massage, a manicure and pedicure. After I left there, the driver took me to a salon where my hairdresser gave me the prettiest set of romantic curls that made my shoulder length hair look fabulous. My stylist then excused herself. When she re-emerged, she came from the back with a dress and shoes.

"What is this?" I asked.

"For you. Your husband had these items sent here for you to put on right now."

"Girl, what does my husband have planned?" I curiously asked.

"I have no clue. He only instructed me to have you put this outfit on and that's all I know." She winked at me. I retrieved the dress and she led me to a private room. I put on everything then I stood in front of the full length mirror to take in my appearance. In my opinion, I looked good enough to be served on a platter myself but I would leave that up to Donovan. The St. John Satin Bodice and Bonded Lace Dress I wore accentuated every curve of my body yet gave me the sophistication of Michelle Obama.

"Denise, you look great but we must get you going or you're going to be late for the next part of your day." She ushered me to the door and held it open so I could walk back to the limo.

"So where are you taking me to next?" I asked the limo driver.

"Mr. Rodgers instructed me not to tell you. You'll just have to go along for the ride and see."

"Okay." I smiled from ear to ear. My stomach was in knots the entire ride. I had no clue where we were headed until we started to going in the direction of my home.

"It looks like we're going home." I said but the driver didn't answer me. He just politely smiled in the rearview mirror. We did in fact pull up to my house and there were several cars parked in our driveway. I started to get confused.

"What's going on here?" I inquired. Then, as if some synchronized move, the driver pulled out his cell phone and made a call. When he hung up, I saw my husband come out of the house wearing a suit and tie. I smiled as he approached the limo. The driver then got out and opened the door for me. Donovan helped me out of the vehicle.

"I'm gonna get you! What is going on here, baby?"

"This is the final part of my surprise. You look so beautiful, honey." Donovan spun me around to see my entire outfit.

"Thank you. You have some serious taste. This dress fits me perfectly."

"Well I know fashion like I know my woman. Like the back of my hand." He winked. "Now we must get inside. I don't want to keep our guests waiting." He linked my arm into his and we began to make our way back inside.

The minute we entered, everyone in attendance started to clap for us as if we were right in the middle of winning an award. I saw a few faces that I knew, like his mother, Shay, and some others from the church with every week. The rest, I didn't know. I had no idea Donovan planned a surprise dinner party for me.

"Baby, I know that we're married but I wanted to plan something special as your official welcome to my life."

"Aww, you're so thoughtful." I replied and continued to smile as photographers snapped pictures of him and I.

As I walked around the room to greet our guests, I heard praises coming from everyone. *Oh my goodness, you look amazing. We're so glad Donovan has finally found him a wife.*

All I could do was smile and thank God that these Florida people were nothing like the haters I faced on a daily basis in Ohio. I took in all the treatment. I quickly got used to it and embraced it.

"Mommy, you look pretty!" Kaylah screamed as she ran up to me and gave me a big hug and kiss.

"Thank you, sweetheart."

"Kaylah is surely right. You look absolutely beautiful," said Joann. She smiled from ear to ear.

"Thank you so much, Ms. Joann."

"I told you to please call me mom. I don't want you to call me anything else."She answered and then I replied, "Ok mom."

I swear Donovan's mother Joann had to be the sweetest woman I had met in my entire life. Since the beginning, she embraced me one hundred percent. She was nothing like Randy's wench of a mother. When Donovan and I first started dating, I used to think she wouldn't accept me since I was divorced and already had a child. But she turned out to be the complete opposite.

I made my way through the room over to Shay, who sat next to one of the under shepherds from our church.

"Shay, I just wanted to personally thank you for

all of the hard work you put in for this dinner. Everything looks amazing!" I reached out and hugged her.

"Well I can't totally take all the credit. Thank God Malcom is back on the team. He's the one who helped me plan everything. Without him, I wouldn't have been able to pull this off for you."

"Malcom is working for Donovan again?" I asked.

"Yes. He came back on about a week ago."

"Oh okay." I replied as I made a mental note to mention this to Donovan later. Then, I looked around the room and saw Malcom. Within fifteen minutes, he worked his way over to where Donovan and I sat.

"Hey newlyweds! I'm sorry I'm late. Denise, you look nice."

I stood up from the table and gave him a hug. I wanted to choke him. He then greeted my husband.

Throughout dinner I tried to concentrate on having a good time but I couldn't help but feel some kind of way about Donovan keeping this from me. Somehow, I didn't feel much in the celebratory mood anymore.

We had just finished saying goodbye to our last three guests when Donovan finally asked, " Babe, are you okay? You seem upset about something."

"Donovan, why didn't you tell me that Malcom was back?" I said as I removed my heels and placed them at the edge of the steps.

"Wait a minute. Who told you that?"

"Shay. When I went to thank her for everything,

she said she couldn't have did it without Malcom. How is this even possible?"

"Malcom came to me and apologized for everything. I can't deny the fact that he is the best assistant I've ever had. We were able to squash our differences. He actually offered to help plan this surprise as sort of a peace offering between us," Donovan explained.

"Don't you think I deserve to know. Just because he calls himself apologizing to you doesn't make it alright. I can't believe you were going to keep this from me." I turned away to walk up the stairs.

"Where are you going?"

"I don't want to see or talk to you right now." I left him standing in the middle of our foyer.

The next morning, I woke up and realized Donovan never came to bed. I found him in his walk-in closet pulling suits out.

"What are you doing?" I asked.

"Getting my suits that need cleaning. I'm going to Atlanta this weekend."

"Oh yeah, I forgot Atlanta was this weekend."

"I would've woke you up but I didn't want to disturb you. Can you do me a favor and drop these off for me?"

"Sure."

He walked over and kissed me on the cheek.

"Thanks, baby. You're the best. I'm getting ready to leave for Atlanta shortly. I have to stop down by the church and grab something. I appreciate you and I promise that you and Malcom will get along. Just give it a little time. That's all."

"If you say so."

After I got Kaylah up and dressed, I figured it would be a good time to drop his suits off at the cleaners. I actually had a few items to take as well. I retrieved his suits and then laid them across the bed. I started to check all of his pockets to make sure he didn't have anything in them. There was nothing worse than ruining expensive clothing because a piece of gum or a pen left in one of his pockets. Most were clear until I got to his last suit jacket on the bed. I found a letter written to him on a piece of notebook paper. It was folded very neatly. I put it to my nose and sniffed it, seeing if I smelled a trace of perfume. Donovan's cologne was all over it. I opened the letter and began to read.

Donovan,

I just can't believe that you passed me up to have a relationship with her. You know what we had was real and I should be the one in her place. You're marrying a woman you don't even know and I was the one who held you down the entire time. And you know what's crazy I try so hard to hate you because of everything you've done to me but no matter how hard I've tried, I must admit I still love you and I am still in love with you. I honestly don't think there is anything you could ever do to make me not love you. It's ok. I'll let you play with Denise for a little while and, when you get tired of her and you're ready to be with the one who has always truly loved you then you, know where to find me.

Love you always,

Sweets

I became so enraged that I almost ripped it up. I started to feel like if it wasn't one damn thing, it was another. The other things I've discovered along the way were considered faulty but this was the first piece of information that I felt was concrete evidence that something else was going on. My heart started to pick up its pace as I stared at this piece of paper that he didn't expect for me to ever find. I felt like smoke was fuming from my nostrils. It was clear to see that he had something secretive going on with someone other than me and now I was staring at the actual proof. It was beginning to get harder and harder for me to believe that he was on the up and up. I was pissed that he had left to go out of town for the weekend. That meant I had to wait the entire weekend just to confront his ass about this. Finding these types of things only further confirmed my decision to continue keeping my pregnancy a secret from him. Getting an abortion looked more and more attractive with each day that passed.

Chapter 15

Denise

Since Donovan went to Atlanta for the weekend, I decided to do what I do best, shop till I dropped. I figured that would make me feel better. I didn't call Shay to accompany me this time, I needed to be alone.

I made a trip to *The Mall at Millenia* and went in and out of stores until I literally got tired of swiping my card. Security had to escort me to the car and help me carry all my bags. Usually this would've made me so happy but, deep down inside, I couldn't feel more horrible. I needed to talk to my best friend. I pressed the face time function on my iPhone and prayed Terri picked up. I pressed the end button when I heard her voicemail come on. I wasn't in the mood to leave a voicemail.

With Donovan being gone for the past few days

all I could think about is the baby that was still growing inside of me. I know that he would be ecstatic to know that I carried his child because starting a family is all he talked about but I still felt apprehensive about having another child. Especially, since there were a few things that I have found out about him that has made me quite suspicious. Thank God that I still wasn't showing. I would literally die if he actually caught on to the fact that I was with child. It would be better for me if he didn't notice anything that way I can go and have the procedure done and he wouldn't have a clue. While I'm recuperating, I can play the entire scenario out as if I have the flu or a stomach bug or something and everything will be fine. I pulled up the number of the clinic that I googled and dialed the number. I ended up getting their voicemail and I hung up. I could've left a message for them to call me back but that would've been too tricky of a move. It would be my luck that they would call me when my husband happened to be near my phone and then my plan would be over. I figured I would call them back and take care of things at another time.

I took notice of the time and noticed that it was already four o'clock and Donovan had text me to let me know his flight would land in about three hours. I planned on having an open and honest talk with him. I planned to sit down with him in a calm manner and get him to talk to me about what's going on. I had three hours to get my thoughts together, three hours to calm my anger down so that I wouldn't fly off the handle and also three hours until I hopefully heard the honest truth from my husband.

When Donovan walked through the door, I had

everything I wanted to say to him. He seemed extra bubbly, smiling from ear to ear as if he was Joker from Batman. His disposition threw me off. He obviously appeared as if he had something to say and, before I could even ask, he took me by my hand.

"Baby, I need for you to put your shoes on so we can go."

"Donovan, where are we going? You just got home?" I asked.

"I'm taking you out to dinner. I have some news to share with you and it absolutely cannot wait." He placed a kiss on my hand and I went into the closet just off the foyer and slipped into my classic nude Christian Louboutins. Our nanny pulled up to the house shortly after Donovan came home to watch Kaylah while we went out.

Once we got to the car, he presented me with four red roses.

"Four is such a beautiful number. I just had to give you four red roses." He said as I smiled at him.

"What are you planning to do? What do you have up your sleeve, Mr. Rodgers?"

He didn't say anything until he pulled up in front of the *Grand Bohemian Hotel*. The valet opened the car door and Donovan led me into *The Boheme* Restaurant, located right off the lobby. I had never been there but I definitely loved the upscale, modern theme of the entire space. It gave off a romantic vibe and, even though I wasn't necessarily in the romantic mood, it still allowed me to relax a little so that I could enjoy myself. The hostess appeared to already be expecting us because, as soon as she saw Donovan, she led us back to our table.

"I see you already had all this planned." I tapped him on his arm. He laughed. The waitress brought us water with lemon. Donovan grabbed me by both of my hands as we sat across the table from each other.

" I know you're confused as to why I wanted to rush you out. But I believe good news must be celebrated."

"Okay."

"Remember how I've been going back and forth with Alliance Publishing about a book I have been writing?"

"Yes, I remember. You've been working on that book for months."

"Well, they emailed me while I was out of town. They want to publish my book. In fact, they have just offered me a four million dollar, three book deal." He grabbed my hands even tighter.

"Wow, that is amazing!" I replied as the waitress came to ask us if we needed anything else.

"Yes, can we have a bottle of your finest champagne. This is a cause for a celebration."

I smiled at my husband for what he had just told me and decided that bringing up that measly little letter wasn't exactly important at the moment. It could wait for now.

Chapter 16

Randy

"So how was your trip down to Orlando?' Deacon Russell asked as I sat across from him and his wife Sheila in their living room.

"Deacon, it was a complete disaster. I had to meet the clown of a man she married."

"What do you mean by that?" Sheila asked as she took a sip of her coffee.

"Let's just say the way he is on television, is not the way he is in real life."

"What was he like?" Russell inquired.

"He came off very arrogant and a pure show off. The first day I got there we ended up getting into it over a whole bunch of nothing. Then the next day, he came late to the meet us for lunch and out of the blue, pulled out these boxes from Tiffany's for Denise and Kaylah."

"Why would he do something like that?" Sheila and Russell asked simultaneously.

"To me, it seems liked he was trying to show off. There's just something about him that rubs me the wrong way."

"How was Denise responding to all this?"

"She honestly seemed oblivious to his behavior like she didn't notice anything. Denise thrives off of stuff like that."

"Knowing her, she probably had little stars in her eyes like she was looking at Jesus himself." Sheila rolled her eyes. Ever since our divorce, Sheila has made it a point to voice how much she doesn't like Denise.

"She seemed happy that I had a front row seat to see someone loving her."

"That sounds just like her." She shook her head back and forth.

"I don't know but it's just something about this guy that I can't quite put my finger on."

"Do you think it's something not right about him or did you just personally clash with him?" Russell asked.

"I definitely feel in my spirit that something about him isn't right. My discernment is very strong. I really don't care what he does just as long as he treats my daughter right. Cause if he doesn't, then he will see a side of me he doesn't want to see.

I received a text message from Alexis inviting me over for dinner since we hadn't seen each other in the last few days. I was glad that I would finally be spending some time unwinding with her because that trip to Florida had me more stressed than ever. I was already stressed with having to deal with my daughter being so far away from me and now I had to worry about the clown Denise called her husband. I stopped by the first floral shop I came to and picked up a nice bouquet of red roses. When Alexis answered the door, she appeared all smiles. She just so happened to be wearing my favorite red dress made her look like a runway model.

"Wow. You look amazing. What did I do to deserve you?" I asked as she twirled around in a circle to show off her dress and then playfully kissed me on my lips.

"I don't know but God must really love you to bless you." She busted out laughing and her little fake arrogance caused me to laugh too. For as long as I had known her, she had never been arrogant, so when she made little comments like this, I laughed.

"He sure did. He had mercy on my sorry little soul." I picked her up and held her in my arms.

"I missed you so much while you were gone."

"I missed you too, baby. My trip was crazy." I said as followed her in to the house and we walked to the kitchen where she put her fresh flowers in a vase.

"What happened? Why was it crazy?"

"I really don't even want to get into it right now. I actually just want to unwind and enjoy your presence.

Thats all." I smiled, hoping she wouldn't probe any further.

"It's okay. I understand. I'm just glad you're home."

"What is smelling so good?" I asked as I started to sniff around the kitchen.

"I made you a little something special." She took me by the hand and led me into the dining room where the lights were dim and she had three candles lit in the middle of the table. She served me T-bone steak, scalloped potatoes, and seared asparagus.

"You really know how to welcome your man home. This food tastes delicious. I said as I could barely stop eating to compliment her skills.

"I'm glad you're enjoying it babe." She smiled and then we were interrupted by a sudden knock at the door.

"I wonder who that is?" I asked. Alexis filled our glasses.

"I'm not sure. Maybe they have the wrong apartment." She handed me my glass and sat back down at the table. The person at the door knocked again. She attempted to get up but I stopped her.

"Don't worry babe. I'll get it." I got up and hurried to open the door since the knocking never stopped. When I opened the door, there stood a man with gold fronts in his mouth.

"Is Alexis here?" He asked. The way his nostrils flared and his jaw clenched, he seemed to be upset. Alexis must've heard his voice because the minute she turned the corner and came around to the door, she froze up like she saw a ghost.

Jessica A. Robinson

"Teddy?" She said with a concerned look on her face. I had a feeling our little romantic dinner was officially over. Teddy then walked past me and inside of Alexis apartment. He casually looked around and laughed.

"Oh, I'm sorry. Was I interrupting something?" he asked.

"Actually, you were."

"What are you doing here, Teddy? I thought you were in jail."

Teddy let a smile creep across his face.

"I don't care what you thought. You would've known if you had answered any of my calls."

Alexis sighed and walked past us to shut the door.

"Teddy, I don't know why you're calling me. We don't have anything left to talk about."

"Oh, how we soon forget. We most definitely have things to talk about, otherwise I wouldn't have come all the way from Georgia. It's cool. It seems like you have a little amnesia but I'm not leaving town until you remember and we set things straight. Don't worry, I will leave so y'all enjoy this sorry ass date. Alexis, we will be in touch." Teddy walked out of Alexis apartment leaving the door wide open.

After he left, we tried to get back to where we left off but things between her and I got a little awkward.

"So you didn't know Teddy had been released from jail?" I asked.

"No, not at all. When he started calling me, I just

141

assumed it was one of his friends trying to get in touch with me. Teddy was notorious for sending a message through them. I never thought it was actually him."

"That's crazy, baby. I can't believe he's out of jail and here in Ohio for that matter."

"Me either. This is crazy. It's like my worst nightmare coming true all over again."

"Well, I know that I haven't slept over here but I would definitely stay tonight with you just in case he comes back."

Alexis shook her head no.

"Babe, it's okay. You don't have to stay over here. Teddy may be stupid but he definitely isn't that stupid. He won't be coming back over here. I promise you that. He definitely doesn't want to end up back in jail. With all that has transpired, I think I'm gonna turn in a little early tonight. I'm sorry honey."

"It's okay, baby. I will leave but promise you will call me if he comes back over here. I will be here instantly." I offered and gave her a kiss on the cheek.

As I drove home, I couldn't help but replay the night's events over and over in my head. All that kept repeating in my mind was, *I'm not leaving town until you remember and we set things straight.* I wonder what they had to set straight and why Alexis was so calm with the very man who threatened her life more times than she could count. There were so many things that didn't seem to add up to me but I knew that things would come to light sooner or later. Until now, I couldn't figure out why I had been so hesitant to move forward with Alexis but was glad that we were taking things very slowly. From the looks of things, it appeared as though she had some loose ends to tie up. I'm unsure of how everything will play out between us but one thing is for sure I'm determined not to be in any drama this time around. I would rather be alone.

By the time I reached my front door, Alexis called me. I answered immediately.

"Is everything okay?" I asked but all I could hear was her crying in the background.

"Yes, I'm fine. I'm just tired of Teddy. I never thought he would show up here. I wished he would just let me move on and enjoy my life. And I know everything sounds and looks crazy but I need you to promise me one thing."

"And what is that?" I inquired.

"Please, don't leave me until I have a chance to clear everything up. I just need you to promise me that." She pleaded.

"Okay Alexis you have my word. Just promise me that you will keep everything straight with me and let me in on what's going on."

"I can do that. Well I'm going to get off of here so I can go to bed. And if anything happens just remember that I really do love you with everything I have in me."

"I love you too." I ended my phone call with Alexis and ended up just as confused as I was before I left her house. I didn't know what in the world was going on with Alexis but I prayed she kept her word and made everything straight.

Chapter 17

Terri

When I glanced down at my Rolex watch and realized that it was time to leave the office, my natural reaction was to look at my court cases and figure out what else I could work on so that I didn't have to rush home. There was a point in time when I couldn't wait until the end of the day so I could rush home to spend time with my husband. But, currently, I wasn't that enthused. Ever since Carlos sided with his daughter, my mind has been in another place. I really thought Carlos would see straight through her lies but she actually had convinced him that she was telling the truth.

I lingered around the office for as long as I could. I thought Carlos would beat me home but, as I drove, he had sent me a text message. He said he would be a little late.

Okay babe that's fine. I'll go home and start dinner. Sounds good. See you soon.

I prayed out loud, asking God to help me deal with Lily the way I needed to. I hoped that, when I got home, she had decided to turn over a new leaf so that we could at least get along for time being. When I pulled up, I expected to see her sitting in her favorite spot on the couch in my living room drowning herself in social media. I was surprised I didn't find her sitting there. The volume of her music played loud enough for her to supply the entire block. I didn't bother calling her name. I sat my things down then walked up the steps to her room. Her door was cracked and, from the hallway, I could see her in there kissing some boy. I felt my anger rise from zero to sixty in the matter of seconds. And, before I knew it, I stormed in her room and pushed the door open all the way.

"Lily, what do you think you're doing?" I asked. Just the sound of my voice caused her and him to jump. Their bodies shook as if they saw a ghost.

"Terri, I didn't think you would be coming home right now," Lily answered.

"Listen, it doesn't matter when I come home. This is my house. And who is this?" I pointed to the skinny teenager who quivered in his pants.

"This is my friend Kerry."

"Don't worry. I was just getting ready to leave."

"You darn right you're getting ready to leave. And don't you ever come back!" I hollered as he ran out of

Lily's room and out the house. Once I heard the door slam, I completely lost all composure.

"What in the world was that, Lily? You're not even old enough to have a boyfriend. And then to make matters worse you have some random boy over the house like everything is okay."

"You are so wrong for that Terri. Kerry is my friend. He is not some random boy I don't know."

"He is some random boy and you know it. You don't even live in town and I know you don't know anyone from here so how did you even meet him?"

"I met him from Facebook," she replied.

"You know what? That's it. I'm calling your dad right now." Her attitude turned to desperation.

"Please don't call my dad. He's gonna kill me," she pleaded.

"Maybe that's what you need since you feel like it's okay to disrespect me."

I called Carlos and, when he picked up, I told him we had an immediate problem that needed to be addressed right now. He said he was on his way since he didn't have to stay at work like he thought. The look on Lily's face was priceless. She looked like she was on one of those scared straight programs.

"Terri, please don't tell my dad. I will do anything so I don't get in trouble."

"Anything like what?" I asked.

"I will tell the truth about your shoes and tell daddy

that I did it on purpose. I will say anything just so that I don't get in trouble."

"Just wait until your dad gets here. You can tell him whatever you want to say then." I went downstairs and waited until Carlos came through the door.

"What's going on, honey?" Carlos asked. I held up my finger and then called Lily to come downstairs to the kitchen.

"I came home from work to find Lily with some random boy up in her room, kissing."

"Terri! You promised me you wouldn't tell my dad." Lily plopped down on the couch so hard I thought she would fall straight to the floor.

"I never promised you anything. You promised that you would tell your dad everything that you've done so you wouldn't get in trouble. Friends promise to not tell secrets. I'm not your friend." I looked over at Carlos, who looked like he wanted to put his fist through a wall.

"What were you thinking? I don't even allow you to have a boyfriend, so how did you think having a boy over would be okay." He looked at his daughter.

"He is my friend, dad. I don't know why y'all are tripping. He's just my friend."

"I don't care what you think he is, you're not allowed to have any boyfriends and you definitely aren't allowed to have any boys over here period."

"Okay, daddy."

I definitely wasn't going to let her get off that easy.

"And what else do you have to tell your dad."

Lily paused for a second like she wasn't going to say anything.

"Lily, I'm waiting." Carlos folded his arms and waited on her to open up her mouth and speak again.

"I burned up Terri's shoes on purpose dad." She tried to mumble and whisper her response.

"I didn't hear you. What did you just say?"

"Daddy, I messed up Terri's shoes on purpose."

"I can't believe you right now. You've never acted like this before and now you're out of control. Well, I may not know many things but I do know that you're going to follow me upstairs and we're going to sort all of this stuff out right now!" Carlos warned and started to walk up the stairs.

Lily didn't follow him. Instead she burst into tears.

"Daddy, I'm so sorry. I never meant to act this way. This isn't my fault."

"What do you mean this isn't your fault? And don't you stand here and try to blame it on one of your stupid friends because you're gonna have to deal with me."

" Mommy put me up to all this." Lily blurted out in between tears.

"What?" I asked as my mouth dropped to the kitchen floor.

Carlos stopped dead in his tracks and came back down the stairs.

"She did what?"

"Mommy told me when, I came here, that I didn't have to listen to Ms. Terri. She told me to do things that would make you two argue and she told me to destroy your shoes. I'm sorry, daddy. And I'm sorry, Ms. Terri. I didn't mean for all this to happen. I feel like I just messed everything up."

"It's okay, Lily. I forgive you."

"Don't worry, baby. Follow me. We are going to give your mother a call right now." They both walked upstairs to Lily's room.

I don't know why I didn't pick up on the fact that this was all Estella's evil plans in the first place. It was a shame that she would do whatever she could to try and stand in the way of Carlos and I. I should've known all along this had nothing to do with Lily and everything to do with Carlos. Estella had to be such a bitter woman to even stoop as low as she did in using her own daughter to try and come between us.

When Carlos finished talking with Lily, he found me sitting in our bedroom flipping through channels on my fifty-two inch flat screen. I was pissed yet relieved. I was upset because this was the reason why we had been fighting this entire summer but deep down inside I was relieved that the root of the issue was finally revealed.

"How did everything go?" I asked as I muted the television.

"I just can't believe Estella. I can't understand how someone can use their own child to do wrong. She is one sick woman."

"You said it, not me. But as far as I'm concerned she is sick to use her own child to do something like that."

"I mean, if it's not one thing, it's another. Estella has literally made my life a living hell since day one."

"What did she say when you called her?"

"Of course she tried to deny it but, when I called her out on the fact that our daughter had snitched on her, she couldn't play dumb any longer."

"Wow. You would think after all these years she would just let you move on and be happy, but she insists on making your life miserable."

"Exactly. She gets on my last nerve."

"Well you already know she irritates mine and I've only known her for a short time so I can imagine how you feel. How's Lily?" I asked.

"She's in her room. We had a good talk. I had to explain some things that have occurred between her mother and I. I now think she finally has some understanding about everything."

"Ok that's good. I'm going to go and talk to her for a second." I left our room and walked to the end of the hall and knocked on Lily's door. "I just wanted to come and check on you to see how you were doing."

"I'm doing okay. You probably hate me don't you?" Lily put her head down and began to pick with her chipped finger nail polish.

"No, of course not. I don't hate you, Lily. Not at all. When I married your father, I promised to love, honor, and cherish him. I also hold that same level of respect for you too. There's no way that I can say I love your dad and I don't love you."

"I guess I just feel so bad cuz my mommy said you were gonna be mean to me and only care about my dad and I believed her but now I see that she wasn't telling the truth." Lily said as she started to cry.

"Listen to me. No tears, my dear. This is not your fault at all. You don't have to keep apologizing. I forgive you sweetheart. But now the real work begins. We have to start at the beginning before all this stuff ever happened."

"I would like that." Lily replied.

"Of course it won't happen overnight. We have a lot of work to do but that's why we have forever to work at this. Now give me a hug." I said as we both gave each other a hug. It felt refreshing to know that the truth had been revealed. Now I felt like her and I could finally begin to build a true relationship but even this beautiful moment felt like the calm before the storm.

Chapter 18

Denise

I couldn't believe my eyes when I read the email Randy sent me. He requested that we have a phone conversation about what he'd sent me. I wasn't in the mood to talk to him but figured I may as well get it over with. At least I could try and get an understanding of the foolishness he had the nerve to send me.

"Denise, I'm guessing you got the message."

"Yes, what is this about, Randy?" I asked. I was lightweight annoyed that we were even having this conversation. I swear he lived to try and stumble on information like this just so he could tell me he told me so. Well he was in for a rude awakening because it would be a cold day in hell before I would ever give him that type of satisfaction.

"It was a blog post that I found online." I started to shake my head at the computer screen.

"And you sent me this because…"

"I figured I would bring it to your attention since this news involves your husband."

"So you're telling me that you randomly came across this while surfing on the Internet. I have a hard time believing that since you despise the Internet."

"I don't despise the Internet, Denise. I just don't get on there often."

"My point exactly. So who dug up this information on my husband?" I had a feeling I knew who. I was just waiting on him to confirm it.

"Well, my mother came across it and brought it to my attention," he confessed.

"I knew your mother was behind all of this crap. She's made it very clear that she thinks I'm the scum of the earth. Doesn't she have anything better to do with her time than try to drag my name down any further?"

"Come on. You know how my mom is. Besides, she was initially alarmed due to the fact that our daughter is involved."

"So you actually believe this bull crap random people post online? I swear y'all don't want to see me happy."

"Not usually but, ninety-nine percent of the time, I don't personally know the person in question. And to answer your next comment I do want to see you happy but not if that person is living a lie. What affects you will affect Kaylah."

"Well yeah my husband is a pretty high profile person. People lie on him all the time."

"Okay, Denise you're really starting to sound defensive. All I wanted to do was bring all this to your attention. It's up to you what you will do with it."

"I appreciate the heads up even if it was false."

"Like I said before, my motive was not to anger you any way. I just thought, if there are things out there that involve your husband, you should know."

"Is that all you called for? Because I definitely have better things to do."

"Okay, I will let you go. But, if anything was to ever happen you, know that I tried to tell you first."

"Thanks. Gotta go." I said then ended the call. For a moment, I sat there frozen in front of my computer. There was no way my man could be gay. I mean he is a celebrity in his own right and the public has a way of assuming things and creating things that aren't even true. With a celebrity being so much out in the forefront, they were always a prime target for psychotic people to say all kinds of crazy stuff but that didn't necessarily mean that it was true. Besides, there was no way that I could even believe any blog post like that since it tried to imply that my husband was gay. I couldn't believe what he had emailed me on that fact alone.

The entire afternoon, I couldn't take my eyes off the email Randy sent to me. I hated the fact he even sent it to me in the first place. I had an inkling to dial Mama Tate up and really give her a piece of my mind but I knew that wouldn't do anything but make the situation worse. I definitely didn't have enough energy to talk to Randy for a second time in one day. I wanted to totally erase the email and dismiss the fact that it even existed but I couldn't help to go back to the beginning and think of the first time I met him. Donovan always had impeccable taste when it came to his clothing. He was also very keen on details and such a romantic person. He also had a great eye for decorating. I did little to no redecorating once I moved in. And even with all of those traits, I still didn't believe the man that I married could be gay. There was no way in hell he could be living that lifestyle and I not know about it. My husband didn't possess any other mannerisms that would've suggested he swung that way.

The letters, the mysteriously intercepted phone call, and this blog post had me more confused than anything. I wasn't one to believe other people over my husband by any means but there was no way that I could totally let everything go either. The few instances that caused me to question him were quickly overshadowed by the mirage he created. Time after time he had somehow convinced me that my little discoveries weren't true. As if they were a part of some sort of conspiracy because he was a public figure. I had simply decided to let it go because he made it apparent that we would never see eye to eye on those issues. The more and more I thought about it I decided I would bring this up. I printed out the article and, when he came home for the day, I handed him the piece of paper.

"What is this?" He stared at the folded up piece of

paper.

"It's an article about you. Read it. I think you should know about this." I told him and waited for him to read the entire document.

"So why did you feel it was necessary to give me this crap? You actually think all this is true?" "I'm not saying I think it's true. It was sent to my email anonymously. I just wanted you to see it that's all."

"I just can't believe you. How many times do we have to go through this? You know I live a high profile lifestyle and there are always people trying to make accusations against me. Either you trust me or you don't. Point blank. It's real simple"

"Donovan, this isn't about trust. I just wanted to bring it to your attention."

"So who gave you this article, Denise?" Donovan shook the email back at me.

"That's not really important. What's important is I wanted to bring this to your attention. There are people out here accusing you of being gay."

"Answer my question, Denise. Who sent you this shit?"

I could see his attitude and anger growing. "Donovan, why does it matter? What makes you even assume that someone sent it to me in the first place. This was an article on the Internet. What matters is the fact that people are out here spreading lies about you. Aren't you the least bit concerned about any of that, huh?"

"I am but not as concerned as I am about finding

out who sent you this," Donovan said, as he began to walk closer to me. "Randy sent this to you?" he asked.

"I found it online while I was on my iPad earlier. Now are you happy?"

"Yeah right Denise. I know enough about you to know that you didn't find this randomly on some internet blog site now did Randy send this to you? I'm asking you one more time."

Feeling like I was backed into a corner, I took a deep breath and then blurted out, "Yes, he sent it to me. His mother sent it to him."

"So you're gonna believe your ex husband and what he has to say over me? You have the nerve to bring this bullshit to me when you already know it's not true."

"So you're saying that this article is completely false and there's no truth to it?" I questioned him again.

"It's absolutely false. It's implying that I'm involved in some sort of sexual relationship with another man and that would never be. First of all, I don't believe in that and second of all I'm a man of God who loves my wife. I would never do that to you but, once again, you're paranoid because of what you did and now you think everybody cheats. Well, you're wrong." He took the article and stuffed it in his pocket.

"I really can't believe you just went there."

"Well, if you care about what he has to say so much then maybe you should go back to him." I was at such a loss for words.

"Oh you're quiet? I guess you don't have anything

to say since it's apparent even Randy doesn't want your ass."

"Donovan, you're going too far."

"Don't tell me I'm going too far. I'm tired of being accused of doing things when I'm not." He stood up from the table and made his way back into the kitchen like he was going toward the garage

"Where are you going, Donovan?" I asked.

"I'm going for a drive. I need to leave right now before I say something I regret."His nostrils flared. I actually wasn't in the mood to argue with him so I let him go.

"Okay." He walked out of the kitchen slamming the garage door and I couldn't help but wonder why he was so upset over something that happens to him all the time. If he's used to people spreading rumors and lies about him then why is he so upset now? I was more confused now than ever. Although I had no real evidence to support this accusation, I wondered if there was any truth to it.

Chapter 19

Randy

I had been calling Alexis for the past three days and she hadn't called me back. I texted her and got no response. I even stopped by her house and she wasn't there. I began to worry about her until she popped up unexpectedly at the church while I was working on my sermon for Sunday morning.

"I'm surprised to see you here. I've been worried sick about you for the past few days." I got up from my chair and hugged her. The frustration in my voice resonated. She could tell that I was upset with her.

"I know you've been calling me and I'm so sorry that I haven't responded. That's why I decided to come here and take you out as a peace offering."

"And where are you taking me?" I curiously asked.

"I guess you're gonna have to just come with me and see." She smiled then all of my frustration and anger seemed to vanish. I can work on my sermon later, I thought. Alexis took me by her hand and led me to her car.

"I think you're going to like my surprise." She winked at me and began driving to this mystery location. I had a feeling I knew where she was taking me but I played along and let her surprise me. When she pulled into Millcreek Park, I looked over and smiled at her.

"You remember this?" Alexis asked as she pulled into the parking lot.

"How could I ever forget. We used to come here so much when we were younger."

"You would've thought we lived here." Alexis laughed. We both got out of her car and took that familiar hike up the trail we traveled every day as teenagers. I hadn't been out here in years.

"This trail hasn't changed one bit." I said. Alexis led us to what used to be our favorite spot.

"This brings back so many memories." She smiled.

"If I didn't know any better I would think you're trying to romance me."

"That would be correct," Alexis replied as we walked over to the table and she asked me to sit down. She then pulled out a tablecloth from her picnic basket and began arranging things until everything looked perfect. She lit two candles and then said, "Were you surprised?"

I nodded my head.

"Absolutely. I used to love coming out here with you. We used to have the best times."

"Yes, I used to call this our little slice of heaven. We used to sit here for hours and hours." Alexis grabbed both of my hands and interlocked them with hers.

"You also used to try and take advantage of me out here too." I started to laugh.

"Excuse me. I didn't see you resist my advances so I don't know what you're talking about."

"Well, you have a point. I was willing participant." Alexis then opened up her wooden basket and pulled out the finger foods she had prepared.

"I wanted to bring you out here, not only to reminisce about the old times, but also to tell you something." I became curious.

"I just want to tell you how grateful I am to have you back in my life. Before we got back together, I didn't think my heart could love anyone again. Loving you has changed my mind."

"You already know how grateful I am that we have been reunited. After my relationship with Denise, I definitely appreciate a good woman. And I'm so glad that person is you."

"I would like us to toast."

"What is our toast about?" I inquired. She filled our glasses with sparkling grape juice then handed me one.

"Here's to the good ol' days."

I raised my glass up to hers. "To the good old days."

"When I think about the past, I do have a lot of regrets."

"What do you regret?"

"I regret that I left you and went away. I should have never left. I would've been your wife. We would've been happy and, most of all, I would've never crossed paths with Teddy. I would give anything to go back to the way everything used to be. When our love and lives were simple. My life is far from simple now." Alexis tried to blink back tears.

"I understand that you have regrets, baby, but everything happens for a reason. Regardless of the regrets, we are where we're supposed to be right now." I tried to reassure her but she continued to cry. There was something weighing heavy on her mind and something more she wasn't telling me.

"There are so many things that would've never happened if I never left and went away. I was a different person when I was with him and I did some things that I am really ashamed of." I wiped the tears running down her face.

"You don't have to be ashamed of anything. We all have a past. I have a past. But we can't stay there. It's all about looking toward the future."

She softened her frown and gave me a pretty smile. "Randy, you always know exactly what to say to make me feel better. That's why I love you."

"Now, I remember you said you had something you wanted to tell me?" I stroked the side of her face with my hand.

"Oh, I've said all that I have to say."

"Are you sure, baby?"

Alexis paused and then replied. "Yes I'm sure."

After eating lunch, Alexis dropped me back off at the church and I was able to lock in and finish my sermon in no time. I left the church that evening feeling like a new man. Lunch at the park with my lady proved to be just what the preacher needed. I know things had been strained between us lately due to the fact that her ex-boyfriend showed up out of the blue but I loved this woman and I wasn't going to let some joker from her past affect what we had going on.

I walked out of Oakdale Baptist and noticed that there was a Black Cadillac parked across the street in a vacant lot. I could tell someone sat inside but I couldn't make out the face because the windows were all smoked out. I got in my car and stuck my key in the ignition. Once I started the car, my gas light popped on.

I pulled my S class Mercedes into the first gas station I came to and parked at the pump nearest to the building. I went inside and paid for my gas. As soon as I came out, I saw Teddy leaning up against that same Black Cadillac. He smoked a cigarette. I didn't acknowledge him. I continued walking toward my car like I didn't see him.

"So you in love, huh?" Teddy asked and then proceeded to take a long drag of his cigarette. He looked over at me and laughed.

"Were you following me?" I opened the nozzle on my gas tank and started to pump.

"You're very observant. I like that. Let me ask you something, did you notice me following before you went to your little picnic in the park? Or did you notice me after you left the church because if you pick option A then you're smarter than I think." He blew a mouth full of smoke out in my direction.

"Why are you following me? I have nothing to do with what went on between you and Alexis in the past."

"You do have everything to do with it. More than you know. This chick got you walking around here all in love and you don't even have a clue as to who you've really fallen in love with." Teddy said as he pulled out his ringing phone and silenced it.

"What's that supposed to mean? I know she has a past. We all do and, from the looks of it, you don't exactly look like a former choir boy."

"Wow. Did it take you all day to come up with that line? You're cornier than I thought."

"Whatever, Teddy. Don't you have a crime to go commit or something."

"Like I said, the person you think you're in love with is a totally different person. Far from being your first lady but it's okay. I don't want to spoil your little fairytale but shit is getting ready to hit the fan. If I were you, I wouldn't be buying any engagement rings any time soon. She may not be around to even receive it." Teddy threw his cigarette down on the ground, stomped it out, got in his car and left.

I couldn't help but wonder what Teddy meant by everything he said to me. The way he sounded made me feel like he could potentially threaten Alexis life and I was definitely determined to prevent that from happening. It would be a cold day in Satan's playground before I ever let him lay a finger on her.

Having encountered Teddy for myself made me even more curious as to what was really going on and I was determined to speak with Alexis about my concerns. I had just gotten out of one deceptive marriage and there was no way that I would even consider moving forward with Alexis until I was sure that this situation wouldn't be a repeat from my first marriage.

Chapter 20

Terri

Lord knows I didn't want to go to Texas with my husband to take Lily back home, but this wasn't about me. This was about standing beside my husband as a united front. Although I wasn't trying to make such a big deal out of it, my family and friends were another story. You would've thought my mother was preparing for the battle of Armagaddeon. I think she sent me every scripture she could find that referenced war and fighting a battle. And Denise wasn't any better. She joked about putting aside bail money for me in the event that I got locked up and said she would be on the next red eye flight if I needed her to come and regulate. In my opinion, those two were a bit dramatic but I knew deep down they meant well. Ever since Carlos and I had that huge talk with Lily, I had experienced a totally different child than the one who initially flew out to Ohio with us. I wasn't complaining. I was relieved we had our own personal breakthrough. Now, her mother was a different story but I figured we would cross that bridge when we came to it.

We took that all familiar trip from the airport to Estella's house. I knew I should've said a prayer or something but I found myself preparing for our encounter much like I prepared for a tough court case. I put my game face on and was ready for any venom that evil witch decided to spit at me. When the airport taxi pulled up in her driveway, I took a deep breath and personally decided that I would be ready for whatever came my way.

Estella heard us pull in the driveway because, by the time we unloaded Lily's stuff, she stood in her doorway with the meanest look on her face. She shook her head and mumbled to herself as Carlos brought Lily's luggage on to the porch. Upon first glance, I could tell Estella had an attitude. She opened up the door as we approached. She reached out and pulled Lily into her arms and kissed her.

"Hey baby! I missed you so much while you were gone."

"I missed you too, mama." Estella softened her glare enough to smile and it caught me by surprise. I didn't know someone so mean and evil was even capable of a smile.

"Take your luggage upstairs baby. I'm going to talk to your dad for a second."

Lily nodded her head and disappeared upstairs to her room. After Estella heard her bedroom door slam, she took that as her cue to act a fool.

"So I can't believe you still decided to bring her after the conversation we had last week. You know you never did listen well."

"Estella, what are you talking about? This woman is not just some random person. Terri is my wife. Why wouldn't she come? You're not making any sense."

Estella laughed.

"I'm not making any sense? Carlos I make perfect sense. I thought I made myself perfectly clear when I said that this woman was not welcome in my home again. What just cuz you claim you're married, I'm supposed to allow you to just flaunt your little wifey in front of my face every chance you get. I mean for all that you could've just stuck our daughter on a plane. She's old enough to travel by herself."

"Do you even hear yourself right now? You think I would let my daughter step foot on a plane by herself to travel halfway across the country just so I can protect your feelings? Well I'm not. You constantly bring up the fact that I'm flaunting my wife but I can because we are married and she is my wife. Yes, I know that is hard for you to understand and why you may not accept it, you must respect it. You can be mad all you want to at me and take things out on me like you've always done but I will not let you stand here and continue to disrespect her. That crap ends today. Right here and right now."

"So you don't think that bringing your wife disrespects me? You constantly bring her around intentionally trying to hurt me. Well guess, what you're not the only one that can hurt. I have news for you, Lily is not really your daughter." Estella lowered her voice enough to whisper the last half of what she said. Hearing her confess this news made our mouths drop to the ground.

"What did you just say?" Carlos asked.

"That's right you heard me. Lily is not your real daughter."

"How long have you known this?"

"Actually, I had her tested shortly after she was born. I had my doubts when I got pregnant and sure enough, when I tested her, she turned out to be Ricardo's daughter."

"Why didn't you ever say anything? Why have you kept this a secret for so long? I mean our daughter is practically on her way to high school what makes a person hold on to a secret for such a long time. When were you planning on telling me?" Carlos asked.

I wished he gave me the okay because I would literally fight Estella like I was fighting a man on the street. I couldn't believe she would do my husband like this.

"I didn't think I would ever tell you especially since you decided to step up to the plate and be responsible for Lily and I. But when you chose to leave me high and dry like the way you did, I figured all bets were off." Estella smiled and Carlos attempted to lunge out at her but I grabbed him and pulled him back. I didn't want him to end up getting arrested.

"I swear you are so evil!"

"Come on baby. Let's go. It's time to get out of here." I knew the situation would only escalate from there.

"Yes, it's definitely time to go but I want to say goodbye to my daughter first. Estella you better not ever utter a word of this to my daughter do you understand?" Carlos said.

"Don't worry. My lips are sealed. I just figured you should know the real truth why you trying to run around here and play father and husband of the year." Estella flashed that devious smirk of hers pleased with the drama she just personally created.

I couldn't understand how someone could be so deceitful, I thought.

Carlos was pretty much silent the entire way back to the airport. I tried to open my mouth and say something that I knew would bring him comfort but what could I possibly say at a time like this. We were clear to the airport and I had finally mustered up enough courage to say something.

"Baby, I am so sorry that this has happened. How are you feeling?"

"You know what? I can't even say I'm shocked. When Lily was first born there were rumors circulating around town that she may not be mine but I shrugged off all the negativity. No one wants to hear that their wife has gotten pregnant by some other man. I'm not going to lie. Even as she has grown up I have always looked and tried to see myself in her and I haven't but regardless I know that children can look like members of your family and she favors my mom and sisters. I'm not going to lie. She cut me deep on this one. I am hurt beyond belief and really don't know what else to say at this point. All I can say is that I will remain to be her father like I've always have and I am committed to us moving forward and starting our own family. I can no longer let the evilness that resides in her bitter soul to hinder me from living my life."

I had been so worried that the news that had been revealed would completely crush my husband but he took everything in stride and planned on using it as fuel to continue on with his life. I loved my husband for that.

Chapter 21

Randy

"Alexis we need to talk," I said the minute she opened up her front door.

"Yeah, we definitely need to talk," she replied. I could tell from the moment I walked in, she had an attitude. Something bothered her and I knew the time had come for us to have a serious conversation. We both attempted to speak at the same time.

"I'm sorry, Randy."

"It's okay, Alexis. You have something you want to say?"

"Yes, but I'll let you go first." She said then motioned for us to sit down on her couch.

"Well first, I would like to apologize for being somewhat distant lately. I've been doing a lot of thinking and, the more I think about it, I've come to the conclusion that at this time we are better off as friends. And before you say it, no there's no one else I'm interested in. I just think you and I need to be friends. I've prayed and prayed about this and it wasn't this clear until this morning." I braced myself for her response.

Alexis took a deep breath, exhaled and then said, "Feels like a major weight has been lifted off of my shoulders." Her response caused both of my eyebrows to rise.

"Okay, I wasn't expecting you to say that at all."

"I know you may be shocked, but I've been thinking about this just like you've been thinking about it. I agree. Even though I don't want to admit it, I also feel like it's time for us to part our separate ways. My legal issues with Teddy are not going away any time soon and I really need to solely focus on them and that doesn't mean to drag you along with me while I do so. That's not any fair to you. It really sucks because I am in love with you but, as a result of things of my past, they are taking precedence over everything else. I apologize for even letting it go on this far with you. I wasn't completely honest about the things that occurred between Teddy and I. As a result of some of the choices I made while I was with him, I have to now pay for them. I used to think that running back up here and trying to start a new life would somehow erase all the bad that occurred in my life but, one thing I've learned, you can't run from your issues. At some point, you have to make the decision to deal with them. Right now, it's my time to do just that."

"I understand and feel like that was big of you to say and admit. It takes a lot of courage to do what you just did."

"Teddy has not only pressed charges. The court has issued a warrant out for my arrest and I have to go back down to Georgia and turn myself in."

"Well, once they hear your case, you will be out in no time." I reassured her.

"Randy, I flat out stole money from Teddy. I hate even saying that but it's the truth. I'm looking at major jail time and I'm okay with it. I've prayed and asked God for forgiveness and I'm at peace whatever the outcome is. I knew what I was doing when I did it. That's what I get for getting caught up with a street dude, ya know?" Alexis pulled a tissue from her Kleenex box and wiped away tears.

"It saddens me to hear this Alexis but just know that I will be praying for you and, whatever the outcome, just know that I do love you. I know you're a good woman and I will not sit here and judge you because of your past. We all have one." I opened out my arms and hugged her.

"Randy, I hate that I have to pass an opportunity to be with you up yet again. You are a wonderful man and the next woman who is lucky enough to be with you will be one blessed woman." Alexis gave me the longest kiss.

After she let me go, I jokingly said, "That definitely wasn't a goodbye kiss. That kiss was more like let's go and finish in the bedroom. What you trying to do to me, Alexis?"

We both laughed and she playfully hit my arm.

"Be quiet. I couldn't let our last kiss be a horrible one. Just know if our paths ever cross again there's more where that came from." She winked at me.

Here all this time, I thought that Alexis and I would be able to rekindle what we had so many years ago but some things are better left in the past. Sometimes we try our best to resurrect situations but sooner or later we find out that they are the past for a reason. They are the past because they are meant to be left alone. I had always loved Alexis since we were teenagers and would love more than anything for us to be together but to be honest I was in love with the Alexis I knew from many years ago. So much time has transpired since then that she is in fact a completely different person with her own issues and situations to deal with. No matter how hard I try I cannot save her from anything she's going through. She has to do that on her own without me. At this point in my life, I deserved to be with a woman who provided little to no drama and if that required me to be single a little bit longer than so be it. I was officially back on the market, again.

Chapter 22

Denise

❝I'm still trying to figure out why I'm not accompanying you to New York. It's not like you have a bunch of speaking engagements."

"Babe, there's nothing to figure out. Besides, we've been through this a million times. You won't be able to go with me on every trip and that's okay." He explained and even though I heard what he was saying, I was far from acceptance. There was no reason why I couldn't go with my husband to New York. I was still feeling some kind of way about his reaction to the blog post I showed him. The way he reacted to what I showed him you would've thought that I had written the stupid article myself. That incident happened two and a half weeks ago and he had been trying to get in my good graces ever since. I had completely stopped speaking to him and when he noticed his multiple apologies weren't getting through to me he resorted to showering me with gifts. He ended up having his personal stylist bring me a closet full of outfits, shoes, and handbags. I had everything from Celine, Louboutin, and Tom Ford to my heart's content.

Even though I wanted to stay mad, these highly expensive gifts, made it almost impossible for me to remain that way. I had forgiven him for the time being but hearing him denying me the opportunity to travel with him brought those same kinds of emotions back all over again.

"No it's not okay. There is absolutely no reason why I can't go with you."

"For the hundredth time. I have a lot of meetings scheduled and all kinds of paperwork to complete at the publishing company. This wouldn't be a good trip to bring you on. Besides, you would get bored being stuck in our hotel room all day."

"No, I won't get bored at all. This would be a good time to add to my closet."

"I promise you that the next time I make a trip to New York that you will come with me. We'll even bring Kaylah and make a family trip out of it." Donovan reassured me.

"Okay, I can see that this conversation is going absolutely no where. When is the driver supposed to be arriving to take you to the airport?"

"In about twenty-five minutes. I still have a few more things to pack." He went into the closet and pulled out a few things. He then folded the clothing items and dropped it into his suitcase which was open on our bed.

I sat right next to his luggage flipping through the newest Essence magazine. I would've gotten up to help him but I noticed my ankles were slightly swollen and they hurt to walk on them. I wanted to soak them in some Epsom salt but decided to wait until Donovan left to do so. I couldn't have him asking me any questions.

"So how long is this trip again?" I asked.

"Just for the weekend and I promise I will come straight home to you. When I come home I want you to wear those sexy red shoes that I like." Donovan grabbed at my slipper and it ended up falling on the floor. He noticed something was wrong right away.

"Baby, what's wrong with your ankle? It's really swollen."

"Oh, my ankle rolled over when I was walking in my new stilettos yesterday. I figured it would be a little swollen. That's why I've been wearing my slippers."

Sometimes I surprised my own self at how quick I was able to think on my feet. I definitely wasn't planning on telling him that my ankle was swollen as a result of having a bun in the oven.

"Okay honey. You have to be careful. I can't have my fine, sexy wife breaking her neck trying to walk in heels."

I heard a car horn beep outside our house.

"I think the car is here to take me to the airport."

I helped Donovan carry his carry-on bag to the front door.

"Baby, have a safe flight to New York. Keep me posted on everything." I said as the driver loaded his bag into the car.

"I sure will and I am definitely going to miss you. We're going to go on vacation somewhere when I get back. I'm going to take some time off so we can celebrate. I know this transition has been rough for you." He leaned and gave me a kiss. I reached my arms around his neck and gave him a hug. "I love you so much, Denise."

"I love you too." I went back to the house and made sure he was well down the road then I started to implement my plan. They say that if you go looking for something you will surely find it. Well I was going to look in every nook and cranny of the house until I found something. I made sure my daughter was preoccupied with her toys before I started to search the house from top to bottom. I went through everything in the bedroom and I found nothing. I went through his closet and again I found nothing. I went through his extra luggage and found nothing. I was beginning to get frustrated because if, he was in fact being unfaithful to me, there had to be some type of incriminating evidence to stumble upon. I also went through every piece of mail and random pieces of paper that were scattered all over the house and still I came across nothing. I almost gave up until the idea popped in my head to search his office. Up until this point, I had never really been in his office. I can't believe that I didn't think to go there in the first place. I looked in every drawer, cabinet, on top of his desk, inside the trash and my search yielded nothing. I was getting ready to leave out when I heard his computer make a dinging sound. He received an email. I went over to his desk and sat in his leather office chair. I put my hand on the mouse and moved it across the pad to wake the computer up. To my surprise, he had left it completely unlocked. I quickly scanned over his desktop and noticed that he had two unread messages. I clicked on the newest one.

Mr. Rodgers,

Thank you for your most recent purchase. The custom diamond band you had me create turned out absolutely beautiful. I engraved it with the word "Sweets" just as you requested. I did as you asked and had it sent to your hotel in New York. Thanks for your business. I really hope you enjoy your new ring. Enjoy yourself and congrats on the book deal.

Thanks for your business.

I grew confused after reading this email. This man hadn't been in New York for a good three hours and already he was buying expensive jewelry that he didn't need. I went as far as going on the jeweler's personal website and knew that my husband had just made a major purchase. I'm surprised that he had never mentioned it to me at all. It was obvious that he didn't want me to know what he was spending on such a fine piece of jewelry. The more I thought about it the more uneasy I felt. Why did he feel the need to purchase a custom band? And then have the ring sent to his hotel instead of the house? Something about this whole set up wasn't sitting right with me. I literally felt sick to my stomach. Here I was pregnant with my husband's first child and questioning his every move. I never had to question Randy when we were together. If anything I was the one who needed to be questioned. Now I discovered a piece of information that could be the very key to what I wanted to find out or could be yet another thing that would be spun into the complete opposite. If I wanted to find out the real truth then I needed to do something I had never done before.

I was very tired of Donovan and his sneakiness. And, if sneaky is what he wanted to be, I would give him a run for his money. I already knew what I was about to do. I looked through his other emails until I found his hotel reservations. I entered them into my cell phone. I then got on the internet and booked me the latest flight available to the Big Apple. He wasn't the only one who could dip and dive. He really didn't know who he was messing with. He was about to be in for the surprise of his lifetime.

Shortly after I confirmed my flight, I was able to get Donovan's mom to keep Kaylah. With her being safe and sound, I could totally focus on the task at hand. The driver dropped me off at the airport. I had checked in with security and made it on my plane in an hour and a half. I didn't bother texting Donovan. He hadn't bothered to call me since he left anyway so I figured I would let my surprise speak for me.

I arrived at the *W Hotel* in Times Square and paid the cab driver handsomely. He wore the biggest grin as he walked off with not only the money for my ride but a one hundred dollar tip on top of it. As I stepped out of the cab, the humid night air smacked me square in the face and I started to sweat. I couldn't have entered the building fast enough to take refuge in the air conditioned accommodations.

I walked into the lobby of the hotel and walked straight up to the front desk.

"Excuse me. My name is Denise Rodgers and my husband is staying at this hotel. I'm here to surprise him. Would you mind giving me a spare key?" I politely asked. I hoped she didn't give me any trouble but I knew everything was a go when she started typing something into the computer and handed me a room card.

"Here you go ma'am. His room is on the fifty-fourth floor. Have a good day." She smiled and I was so shocked at how easy it was to gain access to someone's room. I turned my phone on silent and took the elevator up. My anxiety grew with each floor the elevator travelled. My heart started increasing its beat to the point that it felt like it would bust out of my chest. I jumped off the elevator when it got about halfway up. It felt like I was beginning to hyperventilate. I saw a water fountain and I walked up to get a drink so that I wouldn't pass out. My body temperature rose. I tried to calm myself down but, every time I thought about what I was getting ready to do, my heart started racing all over again. There was a mirror that sat directly across from the elevator. I pressed the up button and then checked my appearance while I waited. The humidity had caused my face to have a dewy glow. I pulled a napkin from my Celine bag and dabbed my face until it was dry. Finally, the elevator doors opened and I got back on and pressed the button for the fifty-fourth floor.

Once the elevator doors opened this time, I knew

there was no turning back. I was getting ready to give Donovan the surprise of a lifetime. As I walked down the hall, time began to feel as though it were standing still and everything started moving in slow motion. The mute button had been pressed on any outside noise. I could hear my heart beating, each and every breath I took, and the sound of my six inch heels as they struck the floor all coordinated together like they were a synchronized movement. I walked until I came up on the room that matched the key that the front desk attendant had given me. For a moment, I stood there. And in my indecisiveness, I asked myself, *Do you really want to do this? Do you actually want to know what's on the other side of that door? Do you want to know the real truth?* I took a deep breath and then whispered, "No turning back now." I swiped the key card in the slot for the door and when I saw the green light I turned the knob as quietly as I could and entered.

As soon as I stepped inside the suite, I noticed there were dress clothes thrown all over the floor. It looked as though he dumped his entire suitcase right there and, wherever they fell out, that's where they stayed. My eyes immediately were drawn to the coffee table that sat in the middle of the living room. I started to walk but my shoes seemed to be too loud so I stepped out of my heels and walked as quietly as I could over to the table where I found two empty bottles of Hennesey and a mirror with cocaine sitting on top of it. There was an unfamiliar yet nauseating smell that created a weird aroma in the air.

I heard voices coming from the bedroom and, by the sound of it, I was about ready to catch my husband in the act. They were so consumed that they hadn't heard me come in at all. I tiptoed as softly as I could until I made it through the living room. When I arrived at the bedroom door, I pushed it open with as much force as I could. I flicked on the light and thought my eyes deceived me.

"Donovan? Malcom? What the hell is going on here?" Donovan jumped off of Malcom with the quickness.

"Denise, what are you doing here?" Donovan asked. Malcom got up out of bed to reveal a lace baby doll negligee. My mouth dropped down to the floor.

"Doesn't matter what I'm doing here, I need for you to explain what is going on here." I crossed my arms and waited for him to open his mouth.

"Look, I know what you think you saw but it isn't what you think it is."

I couldn't believe my ears. Here we were in the middle of a New York hotel room and I had just caught his ass in bed with Malcom.

"I don't even know why you're here. We left your pitiful behind back in Orlando where you belong," Malcom said looking like a cracked out transvestite.

"Malcom, I could've sworn I wasn't talking to you. If I were you, I would shut up before I show you where I really come from. If you'll excuse us you can march your little happy ass out of here."

Malcom walked over and stood face to face with me as if he was confronting me on a daytime talk show.

"I'm not going anywhere. If Donovan doesn't want me to leave, I'm not going anywhere." Malcom held up his hand and I noticed he was rocking a brand new diamond band. I could feel my blood boiling.

Donovan then turned to Malcom and said, "Can you please excuse us?"

Malcom threw on his clothes and snarled at me. I tried to run after him but Donovan held me back. "Malcom, can you please leave so we can talk. Alone."

"Please, get off of me," I yelled.

"Denise, let's go in the living room." Donovan attempted to touch the small of my back and guide me. I jerked my body away from him.

"Please don't touch me." I flinched.

"Fine." He sat down on the couch. I sat in the chair at the opposite end of the room. I remained quiet. I was truly at a loss for words. I stared at him as he searched for the right things to say to me. At this point, I don't know what he could say that would make this situation any better. I decided to step up and be the first one to speak.

"You know what? I had an inkling all along that you were cheating on me but never in a million years did I ever believe you were cheating on me with Malcom." I shook my head back and forth. "And I asked you if he was gay. You said no. You are a fucking liar, Donovan."

"Denise, I know all this looks crazy but there's really an explanation for it all."

"I'm waiting on this wonderful explanation of yours." I crossed one leg over the other.

"I'm just sorry that you had to find out like this. You weren't supposed to find out like this."

"You're not sorry. You're sorry that your ass got caught red handed. Let me ask you this how long have you and Malcom been dealing with each other?"

"Denise, does that matter? You're going to be upset regardless."

"Donovan, answer my question."

"Almost two years."

Now everything seemingly made sense. The letters, Malcom's attitude toward me, Donovan's allegiance toward Malcom. That's when it hit me like a sucker punch right in the stomach.

"I feel like I'm going to be sick." I got up from the couch and ran to the bathroom to throw up. After rinsing my mouth, I came back to the living room and sat back down. I imagined my makeup looked horrible. My mascara mixed with my tears and ran down my face.

"Are you okay?" He asked.

"Don't worry about me Donovan. This is unbelievable. I can't believe this. I'm going home. I've saw enough."

Chapter 23

Denise

I started packing my things the minute I touched down in Orlando. Donovan had me messed up if he thought we would be able to make it through this. I was thankful that Kaylah was able to stay with her mother because I didn't waste any time with preparing myself to move. I hadn't heard from Donovan since I left his hotel room in New York three days ago and at this point I honestly didn't care. I needed time away from him so I could calm myself down. I am actually relieved that I never got rid of the condo that I purchased when I first moved to Orlando otherwise I would have to start from square one all over again.

All kinds of thoughts circulated through my head as I gathered my things from around the house. Here I thought that the man that I married would never deceive me. Not only did he cheat on me but to also learn that this same man was also attracted to men stung like someone had poured vinegar on an open wound. I know that what goes around comes around and there is no escaping karma but I never imagined that this is what karma had planned for me.

Now to make matters even worse my daughter is caught up in the middle of this situation. How do I explain to a three year old that her new papa likes men? Or how am I going to break the news to her that we have to move once again. She was already devastated when we moved from Ohio to Florida. And she was getting ready to face a whole new level of disappointment when I had to explain to her that her papa and I were going our separate ways. I just hate the fact that Donovan even has me in this predicament in the first place. I mean don't get me wrong. I've done my dirt in the past but I never expected the payback to hurt like this. This is not even considering the fact that I am now carrying this fool's baby inside of me.

I heard the front door unlock and I continued on with putting some of my personal items in my suitcases in the living room. My stomach felt like butterflies were inside but not the kind you get when you're excited to see someone. The kind of fluttering you experience when you don't want to see a person. I honestly hoped he wouldn't come home until after I moved my things to my place but I guess it's impossible to have everything I want in this life. I planned on ignoring Donovan until I was good and ready to talk to him but when I looked up and saw that Malcom walked in behind him I knew that would be nearly impossible.

"What the hell are you doing here?" I addressed Malcom. Instead of getting in my face like he did the last time I saw him he remained silent. Donovan spoke up instead.

"I felt like an honest talk is long overdue between us."

"No. There's nothing we need to talk about Donovan. I'm getting all my things and I will be gone before you know it." I replied.

"Denise, I know you're still upset but we definitely need to talk." Donovan said as he walked into the living room and stood in front of where I was trying to walk.

"I left New York three days ago and I have not heard or seen you in that amount of time. That doesn't appear to me that you even care that I'm your wife so why should I hear you out now?" I asked. Having a conversation with Donovan was actually the last thing I wanted to do right now.

"Denise, please just hear me out. There are some things that I need to say." I could hear the pleading in his voice. Something told me that he wasn't going to accept no for an answer. I gave him the signal to follow me in our family so we could sit down and talk there.

"Denise, first off I would like to apologize to you. I never meant for any of this to happen. I am sorry from the bottom of my heart."

"How long were you planning on keeping all of this from me? Were you planning on just living a double life forever and prayed you didn't get caught?"

"To be honest I didn't know what I planned to do. I didn't expect to be in limbo between two people. It just kind of happened."

All of a sudden, Malcom felt the need to interject.

"You didn't know what you planned to do? You always told me that you would tell her about what we had going on in time and now you're trying to say you didn't know what you were gonna do? I don't understand where your sudden confusion is coming from. You told me that Denise was your covergirl."

Donovan held up his hand, "Malcom, please let me handle this. I don't need anything extra from you."

I could feel the anger and rage that I experienced from a few days ago slowly coming back. If I wasn't pregnant I would've already been over there at him.

"I just don't get it. If you two were messing around all hot and heavy like this why did you even bring me into this equation? Why did you even pursue me if you were involved with him behind closed doors?"

I observed Donovan taking in a deep breath before he answered me.

"It's very complicated. Malcom and I started seeing each other shortly after he first started working for me. Then you came along. And, for the first time in my life, I saw my chance at traditional love. I wanted to be with you. That's why I pursued you and, while I courted you, Malcom and I were done. I ended things. I felt like it was the right thing to do. But even though I stopped our relationship, the feelings for Malcom remained. It's like I had no control over my attraction toward him."

"So you felt like having a relationship with two people was the way to go huh?"

"No, it's not that. Listen, I've tried to have traditional relationships with women all of which have been unsuccessful. I actually thought that I would never marry but when you came along you changed that for me. I fell in love. That's what people do when they fall in love with someone, they get married."

"But if you call yourself so in love with me, then why would you think it's okay to have a relationship with a man? How long have you been seeing other men?"

"Actually, Malcom is the first man I've ever decided to go there with."

"Well when did your attraction for men start, where you born this way? Did something happen to you that influenced you to be this way?"

"When I was seven years old, my mother's long lost brother decided to come and stay with us. My mother really didn't want him to come and live with us but he didn't give her a choice otherwise. He had done some major jail time and I had always heard my cousins say that he had done time because of touching little boys but it didn't matter to me because I felt like since he was my uncle he would never do that to me. There's no way my uncle would do those horrible things to me because we were family. And for a while, he didn't. It was actually fun having another man in the house. Then slowly, things started to change. We didn't have as much fun as we were previously having. He started looking at me in a different way. He was real serious all the time. He became very obsessed with me in a way that was hard to explain and then one day he made his move while my mom was out of town on business. My life hasn't been the same because of it. I knew what he was doing to me was wrong and should've never happened but there was a part of me that secretly enjoyed it. He created an appetite in me that I've struggled with to this day."

"So you're saying your uncle molested you?"

"Yes. And I tried to forget that all that ever happened between us. I tried to pray these desires away. I've tried to date all kinds of women and erase that part of me out of my existence but it never worked. Malcom came along and saw straight through me. He really got to the heart of what I was dealing with and for once I could just be myself with not worrying about any pretenses or covering up who I was. I believe that's why I was so open when it came to pursuing a relationship with him. I didn't plan on it."

"Oh my God. You're actually in love with Malcom. Did you ever really love me?"

"Yes I love you Denise but... I am also in love with him."

"And they wanted to pay you all this money to write some books. We should've called VH1 and had some damn cameras follow you around. We could've really made some money. I could've been a reality show star." I laughed. Obviously he didn't find what I said funny. I had to laugh to keep from crying.

"I'm glad you find my life funny," he sarcastically replied.

"This is not an easy thing to deal with Donovan so if I can find just a little bit of humor in all of this mess then let me have that at least. I'm really sorry about what happened to you when you were younger but it shouldn't translate into our relationship now."

"This hasn't been easy on us either Denise. I feel sorry for you, I really do. I know you probably don't even believe that but I'm sorry that everything had to come out like this." Malcom said. I looked over at him and then back at Donovan. I really wasn't in the mood to address that fool at all and felt that even speaking to him was a waste of air and my time.

"Oh, I'm completely certain you feel bad for me. Yeah right."

"Do you know that, not only have you placed yourself at risk to contract HIV, you've put me at risk as well. There's no way you can possibly say you love me and be this careless. And God forbid if you've ever been with anyone else. I can look at Malcom and tell he has." Come to think of it Malcom looked fruitier than a bowl of Fruit Loops. I knew this wasn't his first time at the rodeo.

"You don't have to worry about that. We've been careful."

I sighed and threw up my hands. "Oh that's surely a relief."

"So where do we go from here?" He had the nerve to ask.

"What do you mean? I know where I'm going. I'm going straight to my condo that I still own and look for the best divorce lawyer that your money can buy" I answered him. He looked like he was confused about what I just said.

"I am committed to making this marriage work. I'm not trying to end up in divorce court. And you still have your condo? You told me that you sold it." He stated and I shrugged my shoulders.

"Yes, I know what I told you but something told me to hold onto it. I was thinking about putting it on the market recently but I am so glad that I didn't actually do it."

"Well, whatever that's water under the bridge at this point. I'm not trying to get a divorce Denise. I want us to work."

"You cannot be serious right now. Do you see all my stuff in the living room? I'm not staying here. Obviously those drugs you've been taking have you hallucinating."

"Denise, I'm not hallucinating at all. I have a very sober mind and I'm telling you I'm committed to making this work."

"Well, I'm not."

"Listen, I've thought about this long and hard. Divorce is not something that I'm ever going to go through. My parents divorced when I was young and it was the worst thing. Besides, if we get divorced I'm still faced with a dilemma."

"What dilemma?"

"Even though I want to be with Malcom, I can't. At least not out in the open anyway. We have to still hide and sneak around. I've realized having you around as my wife has amazing benefits. You're my cover."

"Wait one minute so now I am your cover. So you're trying to keep me around as some sort of sick arrangement and still be messing around with Malcom too? Uh huh… no. Absolutely not, Donovan. I will not let you make a fool out of me. I'm going to file for divorce." Did he think I was a nut case? Only a complete nut job would fall for something like that.

"If I were you I wouldn't be trying to file for divorce just yet."

"And why is that?" I asked.

"So you think by divorcing me, you won't be a fool? Think about it. Your life would be a living hell. Tabloids, blogs, magazines and everyone else under the sun trying to figure out why you married a gay man. Not to mention all the money I would lose for having to come out of the closet. If my money is affected, then your money is affected. I'm not the only one who has something to lose. So we will definitely not be going to anybody's divorce court. I'm not letting you go that easy."

"So that's it? What's in all this for me? You expect me to stay here and stay married to you fronting like we some happily married couple and you still expect to be sleeping with Malcom on the side and I'm just supposed to grin and bear it?"

"Yes, in so many words. I will still provide for you and keep up with your lifestyle but only we three would know the actual truth."

"Huh, that's interesting. I left something of yours in the bathroom. I will be right back."

It wasn't until that very moment that I knew exactly what direction my life was getting ready to take. I went to the bathroom, retrieved the item I stashed away in the cabinet and then I came back in the room and tossed it Donovan's way.

"What's this for? Looks like a pregnancy test." Donovan concluded.

"You're very observant. Congratulations Daddy!" I smiled as wide as Texas. The looks on both of their faces were priceless. Even though I was hurting inside, my little announcement made this whole moment worth it.

"Wait a minute. You're pregnant?" Malcom asked. His attitude shifted to gloom instantly. It was as if a black cloud was situated right above his head.

"Yes, I am. Donovan aren't you happy? This is what you wanted remember?"

My statement caused Malcom to look at Donovan and he couldn't skate out of this answer.

"You wanted this? You wanted her to get pregnant?" he asked him.

"I mean we talked about this a little while ago. Never expected for this to happen this soon."

"Awww. Don't be so shy honey. You talked about having a baby with me like every other day. I know it's a shock but having your baby must've been in God's plan. I'm so sorry Malcom. I know you wish you were first."

"I can't believe this." Donovan leaned forward and rested his hand on his forehead.

"I know you think our relationship is completely over but it's actually just beginning. Get ready because you two are about to go on a ride."

I had news for them. The old Denise was definitely back.

Donovan did bring up a good point. If I made the move to expose him and leave now, then I would lose way more than his last name and the title. With an offer like that, I would be a complete fool to let that opportunity slip through my fingers. It's something I'm considering.

Holy Deception Discussion Questions

1. Who was your favorite character in Holy Deception and why?

2. What are premonitions and do you believe in them?

3. If your spouse cheated on you with someone of the same sex as them could you remain married to them or would that be immediate grounds for divorce?

4. Was Denise wrong for considering an abortion? If you were in her shoes what would you have done?

5. Do you think that Randy and Denise will eventually get back together?

6. Why do you feel it is so hard for a person to get over people they've dealt with in their past?

7. Was there any scene that totally caught you by surprise?

8. Do you feel that it is possible to be in love with two people at the same time?

9. After reading this book what types of emotions do you feel?

10. Homosexuality is considered a taboo in the church. What are your personal views regarding this?

11. Do you think that Donovan was wrong for not disclosing his sexual preferences to Denise before they got married?

12. What character would you like to see the author write a book about next?

If you would like the author to make an appearance at your next book club meeting please email her at jarlifestyle@gmail.com

Meet Jessica A. Robinson

Jessica A. Robinson has always had an affinity for reading and creatively expressing herself through written word. Imaginative thoughts soon found a home in personal journals. Journal entries soon became short stories. Short stories gave birth to her first novel. This evolution, which started with creative expression quickly, became her passion.

"Initially, I didn't plan on doing anything with my writing. I wrote short stories because I personally enjoyed creating them, I followed my passion for writing and everything else fell into place."

Jessica feels blessed that something that she loves doing has become a craft she can share with the world. Her first novel, Holy Seduction, was released in 2009 by Peace in the Storm Publishing. With the wind beneath her wings from her debut novel, she penned her second, Pretty Skeletons, which was released the following year. Holy Revenge her third novel was the sequel to Holy Seduction. Her forthcoming novel Holy Deception is the trilogy in the Holy series and brings back the characters that you love to hate.

This gifted writer is obedient to her calling of creating stories and situations that readers can relate to. Since the publication of her debut novel, Jessica has won several literary awards and has been features on Black Expressions Top 100 Bestseller List. Jessica is currently working on finishing a few other literary projects.

Passions run deep in this young author. Jessica is a Registered Nurse, and is following her dream of providing care and comfort to patients in the Youngstown, Ohio area while pursuing a Bachelor's Degree in Nursing from Kent State University.